OF LOVE AND LIBRARIES

JUNIPER CREEK GOLDEN YEARS

BOOK TWO

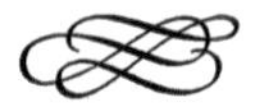

BRENNA BAILEY

BOOKMARTEN PRESS

Published by Bookmarten Press

Of Love and Libraries

ISBN (eBook): 978-1-7781867-4-5
ISBN (paperback): 978-1-7781867-6-9
ISBN (large print paperback): 978-1-7781867-5-2

Cover design by Cover Ever After
Edited by Abby Kendall and Alicia Chantal

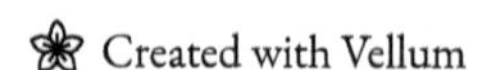

To Orin, the love of my life.
My love for you continues to roam the wilds, getting a little bit bigger each day.

CONTENT WARNING

This book explores the death of a parent and mentions mild homophobia and racism. If these are difficult topics for you, please take the space you need from the story. You matter.

CHAPTER ONE

FRANKIE

Frankie Chan had moved into her cottage in southern France three weeks ago, but she had barely unpacked. The only mark she'd made so far on the cottage was the painting of a crane she'd hung on the wall, which one of her friends had sent her from Hong Kong. And the only clothes she'd worn since arriving were the ones in her suitcase, which was a mess of khaki pants and long-sleeved shirts.

She had little to unpack anyway since she had been traveling for most of her seventy-three years, but she was retired now so it made sense to start settling in. Sitting at the kitchen table, she pulled camera gear out of a box and lined it up on the tabletop.

She shook her head as she pulled out one of her smaller cameras and two lenses. It was unlikely she'd ever use them again, and she should probably give them to one of her photographer friends; she didn't have the energy or the ability to travel for photoshoots like she used to, and she couldn't carry all this gear anymore anyway. She still had three other cameras that she used much more often.

As she picked up her phone to see who would be interested, it rang in her hand, her brother's name flashing on the screen.

"Hello?"

"Hi, Frankie. It's me." His words wobbled slightly. "How are you?"

"I'm alright." She tried to remember when Wing Keung had called last—they usually spoke on the phone once a month to catch up with each other, and she was sure his last call had been less than a month ago. "How are you?"

"Not the best. I have news . . . Are you sitting down?"

As soon as he said those words, Frankie knew what was coming. A sense of relief and loss washed over her. She took a deep breath. "Yes. It's Ma, isn't it?" Her mother had been sick for a while now, and she'd been in the hospital for months. Not that Frankie had visited her.

She hadn't seen or spoken to her mother in fifty years.

"Yes," Wing Keung said. "She passed away this morning."

A silence stretched between them, and Frankie was at a loss for what to say. She settled on "I'm sorry." Her brother had been close to Ma.

"Thank you." He cleared his throat. "Will you come to town for the funeral?"

Her instinct was to say no—she'd been avoiding Juniper Creek for fifty years and had no desire to go back. But she wanted to be there for her brother, and there wasn't an excuse for her staying away from Juniper Creek anymore, now that Ma was gone.

When she was younger, she'd found the town stifling. She couldn't be herself there—she couldn't date girls, she couldn't go on adventures without a car, she couldn't do anything without her mother watching over her shoulder, calling her *Francesca* even when she insisted that her name was Frankie.

But it's not like she would move back there now. She could survive a week or two in town, especially if she visited her friend Margie, who still lived there.

Margie hadn't kept Frankie up to date on Juniper Creek, probably because Frankie had never asked and purposefully changed the topic if it came up. Margie also rarely talked about how she had worked with Ma at the salon—any mention of work on her end had been vague and brief.

There was one other person Frankie wanted to see, too, although she tried to deny it. She knew Dylan still lived there. Wing Keung had become close friends with her somehow, and he'd let details drop over the years. Frankie knew Dylan had three kids, and that they were all grown up and had moved away. And she knew Dylan had been divorced for years and had come out as gay shortly after. Frankie had thought about reaching out multiple times after that news, but she never got the courage. She'd used Ma's presence as an excuse; trying to rekindle her relationship with Dylan would be futile when she would never visit Juniper Creek again.

Not to mention she and Dylan were strangers now.

But now her mother had passed away, and her brother wanted her there for the funeral.

"Yes, I'll be there. When is it?"

"Thank you. Probably next weekend, but I'll call again once we've worked out the details. Would you do me a favor when you're in town?"

Frankie hesitated. "What do you need?"

"Would you be able to clean out Ma's house?" Frankie inhaled sharply—about to firmly say no—when Wing Keung continued, "I don't have the energy for it these days. You're used to moving, traveling. You've kept yourself in shape." He was a few years older than her, and he'd had a desk job for most of his life.

"What about Wai Lun? Can't he help?" Wing Keung's son—Frankie's nephew—lived in Victoria, which wasn't that far from where Wing Keung lived in Vancouver.

"He's on a work trip in Texas."

"Why don't you hire cleaners then?"

"Frankie, please. You know it should be one of us."

"Wing Keung, I haven't been there in fifty years." She'd kept track. "How am I supposed to know what to keep and what to get rid of?"

"That's why you're perfect for the job," he said. "You're not attached to the stuff. The rest of us would probably keep too much." At her silence, he added another, "Please?"

Frankie sighed and got up to go outside, needing the fresh air. The verdant French countryside stretched out before her.

"Alright," she told her brother. "I'll help."

The next thing she knew, she had a plane ticket booked to Canada. But she drew the line at staying in her mother's house. She would help clean it out, but she would not sleep in the house she'd felt caged in.

CHAPTER TWO

DYLAN

Dylan Lavoie watched the stack of books tip over as if in slow motion, and she could do nothing to stop them. That's what she got for using the book cart with the broken wheel.

This was *her* library, and yet everything seemed to be going wrong. The carpet was peeling off the floor, their online systems kept crashing, they'd had a persistent mouse problem, they needed new book carts, and their bathrooms needed an upgrade. As the head librarian, she knew all of this, and yet she couldn't do anything about it without the funds.

The thought of funding did nothing to improve her mood. The library board had suggested closing a few libraries to gain more funding for others, and Dylan was expecting an email from Samaira, the library manager, about their latest meeting. Juniper Creek Library was small, and Dylan suspected the board wouldn't see it as worth keeping open—not if the bigger, busier libraries needed funding as well.

She crouched to gather the books that had fallen off the book cart, her knees complaining at her. Squatting like this couldn't be good for her seventy-one-year-old body.

"Do you need help?"

Dylan jerked her head up and smacked her forehead on the cart shelf. "Shit." She turned to see Evvie standing there, clutching a tote bag full of knitting. The yarn was bright orange, and it went well with Evvie's bright yellow tunic and blue leggings. "For crying out loud, Evvie, can you walk more loudly next time, please?" Dylan asked her best friend.

"Sorry, I didn't realize I was being sneaky."

Dylan dropped the books on the floor again and scowled at them. "Can you help me up?" she grumbled. Evvie reached out a hand, but even with her help it was difficult to get up. Dylan groaned. "I'll ask Gwen to do this. This cart is going to kill me." Gwen was the assistant librarian, and she was young enough to not wreck her knees as she gathered the books. "Want to help me shelve the rest?"

"Sure." Evvie dumped her knitting in one of the comfy reading chairs. "Are you okay? You seem extra grumpy this morning."

"I'm fine," Dylan snapped. At the look on Evvie's face, she sighed. "Sorry. I didn't sleep well."

Evvie's forehead furrowed. "Do you need to see a doctor? You haven't been sleeping well for weeks."

Of course she hadn't—how could she sleep well when her library seemed to be falling apart and the board would soon decide its fate? She didn't tell Evvie that, though; she hadn't told anyone yet, even her fellow librarians. They didn't need to worry.

"I'm fine," Dylan repeated as she parked the wobbly cart at the end of a row, rolling up the sleeves of her blue-and-black plaid shirt. "These are for the YA section."

She was eternally grateful that she no longer had to wear dresses to work like when she first started working at the library decades ago, and that Samaira had relaxed the dress code altogether. Who gave a fuck if Dylan wasn't what people expected from a librarian? Jeans and plaid button-ups were comfortable and practical.

She and Evvie each took an armload of books, slotting them into their spots with the satisfying slide of plastic on plastic.

"So," Evvie said tentatively, moving a few books over, "queer seniors' night is tonight. Would you like to join me?"

Dylan rolled her eyes. "Ev, you know my answer. You ask every week."

"And I'm going to keep asking in case you say yes one time."

"I'm not going to say yes. I have no interest in going to a queer seniors' group." She socialized enough at work. Dylan pushed another book into its place with more force than necessary.

Evvie sighed and put her hands on her hips. "I thought it might be nice for you to meet my other friends, that's all. And maybe take some time for yourself, outside of work."

Dylan raised an eyebrow at her. "Are you sure? Because the first time you asked me to come, you suggested I might find someone to date there. As if I've ever wanted to date."

Evvie widened her eyes innocently and picked up a few more books. "You were married at one point, if I recall correctly."

"Yeah." Dylan barked out a laugh. "And that was a fucking mess. Romance isn't for me, Ev."

"Even though you read so many romance books that you should be planning weddings."

"Ha ha." Fictional romance was the only kind of romance Dylan had been able to handle since her divorce four decades ago. She'd ruined her chance at love in more ways than one, and she'd accepted that. It simplified things. She could focus on her kids and her job without any romance-related drama.

They finished shelving the books in companionable silence, then Evvie went over to her knitting while Dylan asked Gwen to grab the fallen books.

"I'm on it," Gwen said.

Dylan waved in thanks, then went to her office. She always answered the most essential emails in the mornings, and she'd get tetchy if she didn't. Especially lately since she was expecting that email from Samaira.

The paper pumpkin on her office door that said "Let's give 'em pumpkin to talk about" in a large speech bubble did nothing to improve her mood. Her shoulders were stiff as she settled into her chair and moved the computer mouse to wake up the screen.

There it was. The email she had been anticipating and dreading.

She hovered the cursor over the email without clicking it, trying to calm her racing heart.

Her cell phone rang, making her jump. Who was calling now? Evvie was the only person who called her with any regularity, and she was already in the library. Dylan looked at the caller ID and frowned.

She hadn't been expecting a call from Wing Keung, and her stomach sank.

"Hello?" she answered, her voice guarded.

"Hey, it's me," Wing Keung said. He was usually soft-spoken, but there was something in his voice that pushed her anxiety up another notch. "Are you sitting down?"

She was, but she fell back in her chair nonetheless. That sentence didn't precede anything good, and she had a feeling she knew what was coming. "I am. What's wrong?"

"It's Ma. She . . . I got a call this morning. She passed away around six."

"Oh." The word left Dylan's mouth in a whoosh, as if her body couldn't hold air anymore. She pursed her lips as tears pressed at the back of her throat. She had just visited Ms. Wong with Wing Keung and his family last week. They knew this was coming, but the knowledge didn't make it much easier. Dylan had already lost her own parents, and Ms. Wong had been the last parental figure still around for her. "Wing Keung, I'm so sorry."

Wing Keung sighed. "Me too. But I think ninety-eight years old is impressive. If she held on much longer, I don't know that I could have kept visiting her. Anyway . . . I'll let you know when the funeral is."

"Thank you. Can I do anything to help?"

"Not right now. Ma had everything planned out, so there's not much to do at the moment."

"Of course. I'll do whatever needs doing."

"Thank you. By the way, I let Frankie know." He paused. "She'll be in town for the funeral."

Dylan stopped breathing for a second and ran a hand through her short silvery-purple hair. "Okay," she said, her voice sounding strangled. Her hand automatically went to the crane tattoo on her shoulder.

There was a moment of heavy silence before they hung up, and Dylan ran both hands through her hair this time. The funeral would be here in Juniper Creek, since this is where Ms. Wong had lived for most of her life. And now Frankie was coming to town.

Dylan groaned.

Frankie had been her best friend during her formative teenage years. They had met at the library and built a friendship here that shaped Dylan's entire life. She wouldn't be a librarian without Frankie. But the rest of their history was too big of a subject for her to manage. She locked all thoughts of her ex-best friend in a mental box and shoved it behind her list of least favorite books.

She took a moment to get herself together then moved her mouse to wake up her computer again. Her email inbox filled the screen. The email from Samaira was still there, unopened.

Might as well rip off the Band-Aid.

Taking a deep breath, she opened the email. She muttered as she read, "Hope you're doing well . . . blah blah blah . . . the board met . . . yes, yes . . . the following libraries are marked for closure unless we can gain the necessary funds by the end of October." Her heart pounding, Dylan scanned the list.

Her eyes caught on the words "Juniper Creek Library," and her world collapsed.

CHAPTER THREE

FRANKIE

ONE WEEK LATER

Frankie sat in her room in the Bluebell Bed & Breakfast in Juniper Creek, staring at the striped wallpaper. For the past fifteen minutes, she'd been trying to convince herself to go to the diner across the street, but she couldn't get herself to move.

"I'm allowed to be nervous," she whispered to herself. When she was fifty-two, she'd worked with a group of Buddhists who had taught her about the power of affirmations, and she'd stuck with the sayings even as they became popular with New Age groups and more mainstream self-empowerment culture.

Frankie wasn't sure what she had expected when she came back to her childhood home, but everything looked so different on her Uber drive over from the Abbotsford airport. She recognized the gallery by name and there was still a bakery, but the storefronts were new and there were traffic lights where there hadn't been any before. This was not the Juniper Creek she had grown up in, and it was disorienting.

Her heart had pounded as the people on the sidewalk passed

in a blur outside her window. What if she recognized someone? Would they know who she was, and what would she say to them? In a small town like this, people lingered. Younger folks might leave, but they often came back as if the town had a magnetic field that called to people who had lived there.

It had certainly called to Frankie, but she had ignored it. And that call probably came more from a certain person than from the town itself. Even the few times she had visited her brother in Vancouver, which was just over an hour away, she had pretended Juniper Creek didn't exist. She'd gone for coffee a couple of times with Margie in Abbotsford, and that's as close as she got. She wouldn't be here now except for the funeral, and because her brother asked her to help handle the house. To go through Ma's things.

Her stomach grumbled and pulled her back to the present. The diner across the street where Margie suggested they go was new, at least to her—although a good chunk of the town was new to her now. The June Bug diner looked almost like a house from the outside, and she was sure it had been a house when she'd lived here.

She got to her feet and tucked her short silver hair behind her ears. She smoothed down her black jacket and her slightly wrinkled khakis, then she took three steps to the door and rocked back on her heels. Frankie breathed in and out slowly and quietly like she was preparing to take a photo. "My past is not a reflection of my future," she told herself. On her next inhale, she opened the door.

The wallpaper in the hallway was striped like the wallpaper in her room but in a different shade of blue. The wooden stairs creaked under her hiking boots as she went down them.

"Going to the diner for dinner?" Olivia, the owner of the B&B, stood at the welcome podium by the bottom of the stairs, her long reddish-brown hair in a braid over her shoulder. Her dark gray pantsuit made her look like she should be in a fancy three- or four-star hotel, not a quaint B&B in a small town in

British Columbia. It screamed *trying too hard*, but Frankie didn't judge.

"Yes," Frankie said. "You said it's good, right?"

Olivia nodded. "It's a favorite among the locals." She beamed at Frankie.

Frankie took another deep breath in through her nose as she smiled at Olivia. "Perfect." Hopefully *the locals* didn't include Dylan this evening—Frankie wasn't ready for that encounter.

As she headed out the front door, Olivia called, "Let me know if I can help you with anything else!"

The street was quiet; most people were probably having dinner. The sun was starting to set, the air cooling off. Streaks of orange painted the sky, a blush of pink peeking over the tops of the houses. It was officially fall now, but the weather here stubbornly clung to summer. The leaves of the crab apple tree in the Bluebell's front yard were just starting to turn yellow, hinting at the beautiful golden tree it would be in a few weeks.

Frankie walked down the street toward the diner, keeping her eyes wide open in case she saw anyone she knew. One person in particular.

When she got to the diner, she glanced across the street at the one building in all of Juniper Creek she had looked forward to seeing: the library. Seeing it was still there raised her spirits, even if it was closed right now so she couldn't go inside. She had spent hours there as a teenager, researching flora, fauna, and photography. It was where she had met Dylan.

She looked away, trying to stop the nostalgia from growing too strong—it would crush her if she let it—and went into the diner.

The June Bug was busy inside, but there were a few empty tables. Black-and-orange banners were strung along the walls, and a plastic skeleton was propped up at the bar, its hand around a mug. If Frankie weren't so nervous, she would have enjoyed the festive spirit. A woman wearing an apron swung by with a plate and said, "Sit wherever you like!"

Frankie nodded at her and glanced around.

"Frankie!" She turned at the sound of her name to see a woman with short curly gray hair in a bob sitting at a two-person table tucked into a corner. Margie wore a skirt and a matching cardigan, and she looked just like Frankie expected from her video calls. The last time they'd seen each other in person had been at Christmas seven years ago. She'd aged well.

As Frankie walked over, Margie got up and met her with a soft hug. "It's been too long," she said as she stepped back and smiled. "I know you're not back in town for a vacation, but I'm happy to see you."

For the first time since she'd arrived that afternoon, something stirred in Frankie's chest that wasn't anxiety or dread. "I'm happy to see you too. How've you been?"

She sat across from Margie, bouncing her leg under the table and trying to focus on her friend rather than on all the other thoughts racing through her mind about Ma, her brother, the funeral . . . and Dylan.

"I've been doing well. I finished two more paintings since we last spoke. You can see them in person this time instead of me having to send photos."

The thought of being more involved in Margie's life, if only for a few weeks, cheered her up a bit. "I can, and I'm excited to see them."

After a waiter took their orders, Margie said, "So, how does it feel to be back in town?"

Frankie shrugged, her chest growing tight. "It doesn't feel great, to be honest."

Margie nodded and sipped her drink. "Do you think being back here could help?"

"What do you mean?"

As Margie spoke, she looked at the table. "This could be a chance to move forward. Maybe heal the past a bit?"

Frankie bit her lip. Margie was the only person in the world who knew the full reason why Frankie had left fifty years ago.

"Maybe? I'm not sure that it's able to heal." She tried to look at every day as an opportunity, but she wasn't feeling optimistic about this return visit.

Margie shrugged. "You never know."

Although they were in a different setting, the two of them spoke as easily as they did over the phone. Before Frankie knew it, dinner was over and she was back in her room at the B&B, trying not to think about the funeral the next day.

Closing her eyes, she thought, *Negativity has no power over me*. To shift her mind to something positive, she pictured her cottage back in France. Her home now that she had officially retired from working with National Geographic. She'd bought it from one of her photographer friends with the aim of finding peace in her retirement.

Juniper Creek was the opposite of peaceful for her, the past stalking her like a lion seeking its prey. Dinner with Margie had been a welcome distraction, but she couldn't spend every waking moment here with her friend.

The sooner Ma's house was cleaned out and the sooner Frankie could leave, the better.

CHAPTER FOUR

DYLAN

Dylan still had the outfit she had worn to both of her parents' funerals, although it didn't fit her quite the same now; thank goodness she hadn't had to wear it to any friends' funerals yet. The black dress pants were a bit tight around her waist and the shirt felt snug around her shoulders. She sent her three daughters photos of her outfit, and they all signed off on it, so it must not have looked *that* bad.

Dylan's dogs, Darcy and Bingley, were lying on the floor as she poured herself coffee. She'd already fed them breakfast and taken them for a quick walk, so they'd be content to laze around for a while. She used to take them for much longer walks, but her body didn't appreciate that anymore.

As she made herself toast, she thought about Ms. Wong. Before Frankie left, Dylan would have laughed if someone had told her she'd be close to Frankie and Wing Keung's mom. But she'd grown closer to both Ms. Wong and Wing Keung over the years, and she always suspected it had something to do with Frankie's absence. They all missed her, so they went to each other for comfort.

When she finished eating, Dylan polished her black lace-up loafers and put them on. She heaved herself off the couch and stretched, yawning. Even her melatonin supplements hadn't helped her sleep lately.

When Wing Keung had called to tell her about the funeral and she told him about the library, he said, "You'll figure out something. You always do."

She hoped with every fiber of her being that he was right.

Dylan rubbed her eyes and grabbed her jacket then hopped in her truck. She could have walked to the library, but she didn't want to get sweaty before the funeral. The weather had yet to get the memo that it was now officially fall.

Story time was on when Dylan walked in, Gwen singing about a giraffe and stretching up high as a few kids on the carpet in front of her mimicked her movements or jumped around half-heartedly. It was amusing to watch such a quiet woman put herself out there in front of so many kids and parents. She was in her element.

Hugo stood at the front desk, his dark brown hands flying over the keyboard. As the technologically savvy one in their crew, he was likely doing something complex that would fly right over Dylan's head. The library catalogue would be a mess without him, and Dylan couldn't remember how they had survived before they hired him three years ago.

"How's it going?" she asked as she approached him.

He flicked his gaze up to her then back to the computer screen. "The system's being buggy again this morning. We might have to take it offline for a bit and record checkouts the old-fashioned way until I can get it fixed."

"Why doesn't that surprise me?" she muttered.

"I'm pretty sure I can fix it, though," he said. "Don't worry about it." He paused and looked up, taking in Dylan's formal wear. "Aren't you going to a funeral?"

"Yeah. I wanted to stop in and make sure everything was alright, though. It feels weird to not be working today." Dylan usually worked at least a half-day on Saturdays.

"We've got everything covered," Hugo said. "Don't even think about work today, okay?"

She sighed. "Okay." If she was being honest with herself, she was here to procrastinate going to the funeral. She wanted to celebrate Ms. Wong's life and be there for Wing Keung, but . . . Frankie would be there too.

Frankie, whom she hadn't seen in fifty years but had once known almost better than she knew herself. Frankie, who had the most beautiful laugh Dylan had ever heard. Frankie, who left without a word right after Dylan told her she was engaged. Frankie, the woman Dylan realized—a decade too late—she had been in love with.

Christ, it was going to be a long day.

Without letting herself think too much, Dylan hopped back in her truck and drove to the church. She didn't recognize most of Wing Keung's relatives, but there were many townspeople there as well; Ms. Wong had owned the only hair salon in town for years, and she had been highly respected as a result.

"Good morning," Evvie said, coming over and linking arms with Dylan. She wore a simple black dress and black leggings. "How are you?"

"Fine," Dylan replied. And she was. She was sad, of course, but she was ready to support Wing Keung and celebrate Ms. Wong.

Wing Keung had insisted that Dylan sit with him in one of the two rows reserved for family at the front, so she made her way down the aisle with Evvie. Evvie broke away from her to sit with Margie, and Dylan continued toward where Wing Keung sat with Shirley, his wife. Dylan's heart pounded as she looked for anyone resembling Frankie, but Wing Keung and Shirley were the only two people currently sitting in the row.

Wing Keung stood and gave her a hug. "Thank you for being here," he said, squeezing her shoulders.

"Where else would I be?" She smiled and gave Shirley a hug as well before sitting beside her.

A few minutes later, while Dylan looked through the program, she heard Wing Keung say, "There you are. Everything okay?"

She looked up to see a woman sit next to him . . . and that woman looked oddly familiar. She had a brown satchel slung across her body over a smart-looking blazer, and she was strangling the strap, twisting it between her palms.

A split second later, her identity clicked in Dylan's mind.

Dylan's vision seemed to zoom in and out for a second. "Frankie?" she said breathlessly, like the name had been punched out of her.

Frankie leaned forward slightly, to see around Wing Keung and Shirley, and stared at Dylan with wide eyes; Dylan suspected her own expression looked similar. The last time Dylan had seen her in person, Frankie's dark hair had been long enough that it sometimes got caught in her armpits. She knew Frankie had changed—her headshot for National Geographic showed her with long silvery hair, which is how Dylan had been picturing her. Now she had a silver feathered pixie haircut that made her face look rounder.

But it was still her. It was still Frankie.

"Hi," Frankie said, letting go of her satchel strap long enough to give a small wave.

That was all the interaction they had time for before the service began.

Dylan found it difficult to focus on the service when Frankie was *right there.* What had Frankie's life been like for the past five decades? Dylan had followed her National Geographic career over the years, and Wing Keung was always telling her what a great life Frankie had, but Dylan could never bring herself to reach out and call. Or even email.

Frankie had left without a word right after Dylan shared what she thought was some of the best news of her life. Dylan had never been able to fully get over that. Especially after she realized what Frankie had truly meant to her.

Who was Frankie now? Would Dylan even be able to hold a conversation with her?

She thought she wouldn't have a choice when the service finished, but the two of them never got a moment alone. The one time they were in the same circle of people, Wing Keung, Shirley, and Evvie held up the conversation while Dylan tried not to stare at Frankie too much. Now that she recognized her, she seemed so familiar that it was unreal.

Evvie tapped her shoulder, getting her attention. "Are you okay?"

"What? Yeah, I'm fine."

Evvie narrowed her eyes at Dylan; of course she knew something was going on, but Dylan wasn't about to bring it up in front of Wing Keung, Shirley, and Frankie. "If you say so. I need to get going. I'll call you tomorrow?" Even to attend a funeral, Evvie couldn't get a full day off from her job at the animal clinic.

Dylan nodded, and when she turned back, Frankie and Wing Keung were gone, pulled into a different conversation.

The rest of the day was a whirlwind, and although Dylan caught glimpses of Frankie here and there, the two of them never got the chance to talk.

Dylan didn't even know if she wanted to.

CHAPTER FIVE

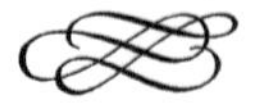

FRANKIE

Frankie stood on the concrete steps at the front of the church before the service.

She paused and closed her eyes, taking a moment to feel the breath of cool wind on her face. The weather seemed too neutral for a funeral. In her travels, Frankie had seen more death than she'd anticipated—animal death, not human death, although that didn't make it much easier. Pop culture often portrayed death as something cold and biting, but it could be sweltering and suffocating as well. A balmy fall day felt too calm. Too pleasant.

Glancing around, Frankie saw many townspeople and a few relatives, but no one she knew enough to say hello to. Margie was giving a speech, so she would be here somewhere, but Frankie couldn't find her outside. She shook her head and focused on her breathing then climbed the steps into the church building. It smelled a bit stale in here, like the carpets needed a good cleaning. Bland instrumental music floated out from the auditorium.

"Frankie!" Wing Keung came over and gave her a stiff hug. Even though he seemed smaller than he used to be, he was still taller than her. His cologne was too strong and made her eyes water, as usual. She'd let him think it was her grief. "How was your flight? How's the jet lag?"

"Not too bad," she said, her words nasally as she tried to breathe solely through her mouth.

He squeezed her arm and she sighed, leaning into that small bit of comfort.

"I saved you a seat beside me," he said, and a rush of gratitude traveled from her stomach to her throat so that she couldn't speak. She wasn't averse to talking to strangers, but talking to family she only sort-of knew and acquaintances from the town she grew up in was another thing altogether.

As she followed her brother into the auditorium, Frankie took in everything around her with a sort of numbness: the casket; the white flowers and the incense on a table in front of it; the photo of her mom with her name, Wong Sau Ying, in script underneath it; and all the people milling around. A few family members she had spoken to once or twice in her life said hello to Wing Keung and nodded to her. She wondered if they even knew who she was.

She grabbed her brother's arm. "I need a minute."

Turning, she fled down the aisle and into the foyer, beelining for the bathroom. Standing at the sink, she splashed her face, looking in the mirror and taking deep breaths. Being back here was overwhelming, and fifty years hadn't dulled her memories as much as she'd hoped.

Once she felt more collected, she made her way back to her seat.

It would have been a relief to finally sit down, except for the person sitting beside Shirley. Even with so many years between them, Frankie knew who she was: Dylan. It felt as if a mild electric shock started at her toes and traveled up through her body. Dylan had silvery-purple hair cut in a fade, only the top left longer; it was nothing like the brown shag she'd had when Frankie had left, and she didn't look at all how Frankie had expected, but Frankie knew it was her all the same. She'd recognize those eyes anywhere.

But would Dylan know who she was?

"Frankie?"

Apparently, yes. Frankie leaned forward slightly, waving awkwardly. "Hi."

A tingling feeling spread over Frankie's shoulders and stayed there for the entire service. She was entirely too aware of Dylan sitting only three chairs over from her.

It hurt that she knew next to nothing about a woman she had once been so close to, but that's how life had gone. She took a deep breath and centered herself. Now was not the time to dwell on the past and what could have been. She was at her mother's funeral.

She didn't cry. She felt like she should, like she was a horrible daughter because she wasn't crying. But she hadn't spoken to her mother in fifty years. Oddly, this didn't seem like a crying occasion anyway. In Wing Keung's speech about their mother, he talked about how dedicated, hardworking, and committed she was. He managed to make everyone laugh a few times, even Frankie, which distanced her further from the person she was here to mourn. There had been nothing funny about her relationship with Ma.

After Wing Keung spoke, it was time for Margie's speech; she must have been sitting on the opposite side of the auditorium. As Margie described working at the salon with Ma, Frankie frowned. Margie talked about how caring and kind Ma was, how she'd give treats to all the kids and truly listen to people's problems as they sat in her chair. This was not the Ma Frankie knew by any stretch of the imagination.

Frankie believed that every photo told a story, but the woman who smiled at her from the photo at the front was almost a stranger, and judging from what everyone was saying about her, she had become someone profoundly different since Frankie had left. What was Ma's story? Frankie examined her photo more, how it showed the wrinkles in Ma's face and her reluctant smile. There was a story there, in every line—there had to be—but it eluded Frankie. Yet she was going to go through all Ma's things in the next few weeks. The absurdity of the situation almost made her laugh.

The rest of the day crawled by, and Frankie said next to nothing to anyone but Margie, even when Dylan was in the same conversation as her. What did you say to the best friend you left decades ago? When a cousin pulled her away into a different conversation, she almost thanked them.

She tried to pay attention to the details as the day went on to keep herself present: The casket being lowered into the ground, the white flower petals on top fluttering gently in the wind. Her brother holding her hand tightly as they sang "Amazing Grace," his palm dry and frail. Dinner at a Chinese restaurant in Abbotsford, one of her relatives passing her a plate with an entire glistening fish on it. The expression on Dylan's face when she realized who Frankie was. The way Dylan had said her name, like it was a wish on the wind.

Now, Frankie rolled over in her creaky bed at the Bluebell and looked at her hands, at the age spots and wrinkles on her skin. How could she still feel this strongly for someone when so many years had passed? And how convoluted was it that on the day of her mother's funeral, her thoughts were dominated by the presence of a woman she had loved ages ago?

She had distanced herself from everyone and everything she knew growing up and had made a new life for herself exploring and taking photos, learning about the many rich cultures of the world. She had been a National Geographic photographer. But being back here made her feel like a kid again, like she was eleven years old and her mother had just moved them here to get away from the redevelopment projects in Vancouver's Chinatown. She was out of her element, and she felt exposed.

This town had smothered her once, and it seemed happy to do so again.

CHAPTER SIX

DYLAN

Dylan called her daughters on Sunday morning to check in and see how everyone was doing. Once she was assured that her family was all doing well and had everything they needed, she could relax a bit.

She would have been able to relax more if the library closure wasn't hanging over her head. It didn't help that today was October 1. Only thirty days left to find a large sum of money to save her job and everything she believed in.

She was lying on the couch in her living room, staring at the ceiling, when her phone rang. The caller ID read "Ev." Dylan reached over to grab the phone, knocking two pillows off the couch in the process.

"Hey," she said.

"How are you doing?" Evvie asked, her voice packed full of compassion as if Dylan's mother had passed away, not Wing Keung's.

Dylan rolled onto her back again. "Tired," she said.

Evvie hummed empathetically. "You don't have to come to dinner tonight if you don't have the energy. I can imagine how difficult this weekend was for you."

"No, I want to come for dinner. I want to see Minnie and

Eleanor and hear about their adventures in the bonnie land of lochs and thistles."

Evvie laughed softly. "I'm sure they'll be happy to see you. I didn't mention the library at all. I thought you should be the one to tell them."

Dylan flung an arm over her eyes. "Fuck, probably. Thanks."

Last weekend, Dylan had called Evvie to tell her about the library. Besides being her best friend, Evvie was the chair of the Friends of the Library, so she needed to know what was going on. "Son of a motherless goat!" she'd said in her typical Evvie way. After a string of swears that weren't quite swears, she added, "We'll figure out something. You'll see."

Everyone seemed to have much more confidence on that front than Dylan did.

"And . . . did you get to talk to Frankie?" Evvie asked now, her tone careful. Evvie and Dylan had been best friends for over three decades, which meant Evvie was one of the few people who knew the full story of Dylan and Frankie's relationship.

"No," Dylan said, sighing. She'd probably acted like a fucking fool when she saw Frankie at the funeral, but Frankie would likely jet out of town as soon as she could, so there was no point in dwelling on that interaction or any other.

"Oh. I'm sorry."

"Don't be. I don't even know what I'd say to her."

"Okay." Evvie paused, leaving room for Dylan to say something, but Dylan didn't have anything to add about Frankie. After a moment, Evvie said, "Well, I'll see you tonight."

After she hung up, Dylan rolled onto her side. She could use a nice long nap before going out again.

Dinner was on the stove when Dylan arrived at Evvie's. She unclipped Darcy's and Bingley's leashes and let them roam free in

Evvie's house; they both jumped onto her sofa and settled at either end as they usually did.

Evvie stood in the kitchen, leaning over the pot of bubbling soup as she added a dash of cinnamon and nutmeg. She wore an orange tunic patterned with bats over a pair of purple leggings.

"That smells amazing," Dylan said, coming to stand beside her friend.

"It's pumpkin," Evvie said, smiling brightly. "And it's going to be perfect with this." She grabbed a loaf of bread off the counter, the label reading "Dawood Bakery."

"I'll slice it," Dylan said, grabbing a cutting board.

The doorbell rang. "There's Minnie and Eleanor!" Evvie sang, dancing over to the front door and opening it.

"Evvie, dearie, you're a sight for sore eyes," Eleanor said. Her Scottish accent seemed stronger somehow, even though she'd only been back in her home country for two weeks. "And there's Dylan!"

Eleanor swept into the kitchen and held her arms open to Dylan, her soft vanilla scent floating in the air around them as they hugged. She wore a long brown dress that seemed perfect for fall. She always looked like she had drifted straight out of a boho fashion magazine, and apparently jet lag didn't affect her sense of style.

"Hello," Minnie said from the doorway, giving Dylan a wave. "How are you?"

"How are we?" Evvie broke in, rushing forward to keep stirring the soup. "Never mind that. Tell us all about Scotland!"

"Let us get our bearings first," Eleanor said, laughing.

As the four of them finished making dinner and setting the table, Eleanor and Minnie told Evvie and Dylan about their trip.

"I had to get compression socks," Minnie said as she dipped a piece of bread in her soup. "I thought I walked a lot here, but Eleanor had us doing a marathon almost every day."

Eleanor rolled her eyes. "Not quite. But you enjoyed it all, didn't you?"

Minnie looked at Eleanor, affection swimming in her eyes. "Of course, love."

Evvie waggled her eyebrows at Dylan, who scoffed. Eleanor and Minnie were still in their honeymoon phase, and Dylan had forgotten how obnoxious that could be.

"So," Minnie said, "what did we miss while we were gone?"

Dylan paused with a spoonful of soup in her mouth. Now was the perfect time to tell her friends about the library, but maybe it wouldn't be real if she didn't talk about it. Putting the situation into words meant that it was actually happening.

She swallowed. "Well . . ."

Eleanor frowned, looking from Evvie to Dylan and back to Evvie. "What is it? What's happened?"

Dylan sighed and put her spoon into her bowl with a *clink*. A splash landed on her jeans, and she rubbed at it with her napkin. "We should have broken out the wine for this conversation," she said to Evvie. She took a breath then continued, "I got an email from the library board. We've been struggling to get enough funds for a while now; the number of library patrons has dropped, and our building is old and needs upgrades. We've been hanging on by our fingernails, but the Regional Library Board met a few weeks ago and decided to close up to five libraries in order to save others." Her throat tightened, and she looked into her soup as she said, "Juniper Creek Library is on the list of possible closures."

There was another *clink* as one of the other ladies dropped her spoon.

"No," Minnie said softly in disbelief. When Dylan looked up, Minnie had her hand over her mouth. "The library has been a key part of Juniper Creek for as long as I can remember. My mother used to take me there when I was a child . . . and that was a good sixty-plus years ago. Why would they close it now? It still sees a lot of use, doesn't it?" She reached for Eleanor's hand.

"It does," Dylan said. "But not enough, apparently. There are a lot of libraries in the Fraser Valley, and I guess ours isn't big enough or important enough to keep open unless we can find money for it by the end of October."

"I've thought of appealing to the board," Evvie said, wiping her mouth with a napkin. "But I'm not sure what good it would do. Even if we argue that our library is worth keeping open, we'd be dooming another library to closure."

"Do you have a Friends of the Library program?" Eleanor asked. "Aren't those meant to raise funds?"

"We do," Evvie said. "I'm the chair for it. We run a puzzle drive in February, and we have a few regular events in place like the book donation bin, the Adopt-A-Book program, and the annual book sale in May. Clearly, that hasn't been enough."

Eleanor nodded, her brow furrowed. "So, we need to fundraise another way. Something extra."

Dylan ran a hand through her hair and pushed her plate away. She'd lost her appetite. "I've been looking up ways we can fundraise: book sales, silent auctions, asking for donations . . . But we only have a month. Whatever we do has to be planned quickly, and I'm not sure it'll gain much traction with Pumpkin Days going on."

"Pumpkin Days?" Eleanor looked at the three of them in turn, frowning. She had moved to Juniper Creek in June and hadn't yet experienced the town's many festivals and events.

Evvie got up and grabbed a brochure from the counter, handing it to Eleanor. "It's a sort of fall festival the town holds every year on three consecutive Saturdays in October after the Thanksgiving weekend. On the first Saturday, there are outdoor games hosted in the park. The second Saturday is a town-wide scavenger hunt, and the third Saturday is the Pumpkin Finale, which is kind of like the Sunflower Festival but with pumpkin carving, a haunted house, and a market. It's fun."

Eleanor flipped through the brochure. "It definitely looks fun. So, you think people won't pay attention to any fundraising events because of this?"

Dylan shrugged. "People in this area know about Pumpkin

Days already. They book time off to come here for it, and they expect it to be happening. Any event we hold would probably have lower attendance because it'd be overshadowed."

Minnie leaned forward, her eyes narrowed in thought. "What if we combine the two?"

Evvie sat up straighter. "What do you mean?"

"Lorelai cares about this town, we all know that," Minnie said. Everyone nodded; Juniper Creek had had many effective mayors in Dylan's lifetime, and Lorelai was one of the best. "What if we asked her to combine fundraising for the library with the Pumpkin Days events?"

Damn, Minnie was smarter than Dylan gave her credit for. A spark of hope lit in Dylan's chest, and she tried to tamp it down. Letting hope get too strong was asking for trouble.

"I like where you're going with this, darling," Eleanor said, her eyes sparkling at Minnie as she grasped the amethyst necklace around her neck.

"Me too," Evvie said, wiggling a bit in her seat. "Do you have any specific fundraising ideas in mind?"

"Not really," Minnie said, shrugging. "I haven't had much time to think about it, have I?"

"No, but Dylan has," Evvie said, turning her gaze to her best friend. "What do you think? Would the events you've researched work with the Pumpkin Days events?"

Evvie's voice shone with enthusiasm, and Dylan couldn't help but absorb some of it. "Maybe. I'll call Lorelai tomorrow and see what she thinks. We'll need to get started on planning as soon as we can."

"We'll help you," Eleanor said, pushing a long strand of salt-and-pepper hair behind her ear. "We were the dream team for the Sunflower Festival, so we can pull this off without a problem too. Right?"

Minnie nodded and smiled at Dylan.

"Of course," Evvie said fervently. "No problem. I'll get the rest of the Friends involved. We'll raise more than enough money to save the library."

As they cleaned up dinner and Evvie put the kettle on, Dylan's thoughts swirled with fundraising ideas: raffles, auctions, donations, yard sales, bake sales, sports tournaments . . . The spark of hope in her chest began to grow.

To the esteemed Library Board,

My name is Eleanor Lennox, and I am relatively new to Juniper Creek. I moved here from Scotland in June to be closer to my daughter and my grandchild.

I have always been a bookish person, and I have written a book of my own that has sold fairly well, to my surprise and delight. Books have surrounded me all my life, giving me places to explore and escape to, and teaching me about all kinds of things I would never have learned about otherwise.

When I moved here, I knew I needed to be acquainted with the library because libraries are community hubs. To truly be a citizen of Juniper Creek, I needed to be involved with the library. That proved to be true.

As soon as I walked in, the head librarian made me feel right at home. She is now one of my closest friends here, and I met one of my other closest friends in the library on the same day. The two of them set me up with a library card and invited me to join the book club, and the library has been invaluable to me ever since.

I know that libraries need funds to stay open. I understand that, and I know it is not the fault of the board that the Juniper Creek Library may be closing. But I urge you to think about what will be lost if the library shuts its doors. You will lose value in this community. You will lose a place where people come to be welcomed, to find community and friendship, to learn and have adventures.

I hope it is in your power to stop this from happening.

Sincerely,
Eleanor Lennox

CHAPTER SEVEN

FRANKIE

Frankie laced up her sneakers and headed down the groaning steps of the Bluebell to meet her brother out front. He was taking her out for brunch before he drove back to Vancouver; he said he wanted to talk through things. Shirley had gone back already with one of her friends who had been at the funeral.

That ominous *things* had hung over Frankie's head as she got ready, not making her mood any better. She'd had a foul sleep, tossing and turning and checking the clock every half hour.

"Good morning," Olivia chirped from somewhere downstairs, making Frankie jump as she headed down. She turned to see Olivia sitting on the couch, reading, a cup of coffee steaming on the table in front of her.

"Morning," Frankie replied, forcing cheer into the word.

"How'd you sleep?" Olivia wore floral-printed slacks today and a white button-up blouse.

"Not too bad," Frankie said. Olivia seemed like the type of person to offer her extra fluffy pillows if she told the truth, and Frankie's horrible sleep had nothing to do with the pillows.

"Would you like anything for breakfast? My husband, Dean,

is our chef, and he makes a mean omelet. We've also got tea, coffee, juice . . . whatever you like. And if we don't have it, the grocery store is a two-minute walk. I'm happy to run out for you." She looked like she meant it, her smile so wide that Frankie wondered if it hurt her face.

"I'm okay, thank you," Frankie said. "My brother is taking me out for brunch."

"Well, isn't that sweet," Olivia said, still smiling. "Enjoy!"

Frankie nodded and escaped through the front door, more than happy that Wing Keung was already waiting for her, his silver sedan idling by the curb.

As Frankie slid into the passenger seat, his cologne buffeted her nose once again. The smell was so strong she could taste it, the chemical flavor of cedarwood making her crave strong mint gum.

"Good morning," he said. "How are you today?"

Breathing as little as possible, she said, "I'm alright. Just out of curiosity, why did you pick the Bluebell for me to stay in?"

"I thought you'd enjoy being close to the library."

Her grumpiness crumbled slightly. She opened her mouth to thank him but got a mouthful of cologne-saturated air. Just as she was about to tell him to get going, he put the car into drive and pulled out into the street; she didn't want to be in the car any longer than she needed to be. Why did Wing Keung feel the need to drench himself in the forest?

The drive to the restaurant took over half an hour, to Frankie's chagrin, and she cracked the window with the excuse that she enjoyed the fresh air. The two of them talked about the weather and how the funeral had gone the day before, with Wing Keung carrying most of the conversation. Frankie didn't have much to say besides that she was glad the funeral was over. It didn't feel right to tell her brother that the woman whose life they had celebrated was not the woman Frankie grew up knowing.

The place Wing Keung picked for brunch was called Don's Basement, a small, cozy space with warm yellow walls and industrial-style decor. The waiter who seated them had glasses that took up half their face, their paisley-patterned shirt sleeves rolled up to their elbows. "Coffee to start?" they asked.

"Please," Wing Keung and Frankie said in unison.

Wing Keung smiled. "Some things haven't changed," he said.

They perused the menu, and after they ordered, Frankie pulled her coffee over, inhaling the caramelized scent of the drink. She poured in a creamer packet, watching the white liquid swirl into the brown.

Across from her, Wing Keung sipped his coffee, not saying anything. Silence had never bothered Frankie, and after her horrible sleep she was perfectly fine to wait until he said whatever he had brought her here to say.

She was examining the pipes crisscrossing the ceiling when he broke the silence. "So," he said.

"So," she repeated, raising her mug to her lips.

"How does it feel to be back in Juniper Creek?"

That was not the question she had been expecting. She tilted her head at him. "It's okay. I expected everything to feel more familiar, but most of the shops on Main Street look different. And I haven't seen many people that I recognize, other than Margie." *And Dylan.*

He nodded. "A lot of it has changed since we lived there. It's a different world now in general. We sure weren't carrying these around when you left," he said, picking up his cell phone, which he had put on the table beside his coffee. "I still haven't figured out how to use all the app things, but I have to admit they're useful."

Frankie nodded. Throughout her career as a photographer, technology had changed drastically. She'd been constantly learning new things since she started, and she'd gone through multiple computers, cameras, and photo-editing software in the process.

"Have you been to the house yet?" Wing Keung asked.

Before Frankie could answer, the waiter came by with their plates. Wing Keung had opted for avocado on toast, and Frankie had gone with a classic breakfast. Once the waiter left, she said, "No, I haven't." She put salt and pepper on her eggs to avoid seeing her brother's expression.

The funeral had been the first thing on her to-do list. The house was second, and she hadn't wanted to see it sooner than necessary. She didn't want to see it at all, really, but she had agreed to help clean it out.

"I think it looks the same," Wing Keung said. "Ma had the siding redone once, and she got the windows replaced. But the yard is the same, and nothing much has changed inside besides some updated appliances. She started giving things away when she found out she was sick, so I don't think there will be much for you to do, really."

Frankie swallowed a bite of sausage. "Okay. That's good. Are you coming to help?"

"I can pick up boxes once they're packed, but it's a long way for me to drive. I'd rather handle the paperwork."

Sighing, Frankie said, "Alright."

Wing Keung nibbled on his toast and watched her while he chewed. It was unnerving.

She set down her cutlery and sipped her coffee. "Wing Keung, what is this about? We talk on the phone once a month. I know what you've been doing, you know what I've been doing. So why this?" She waved a hand to encompass the restaurant and the two of them.

"I haven't seen you in person in four years. Isn't it enough for a brother to want to go for a meal with his sister? Especially after our mother's funeral?"

"Yes, I suppose." She picked up her fork again and cut a piece of pancake.

Wing Keung pursed his lips. "You're right, though," he said after a moment. "I did invite you here for a reason."

She paused mid-chew and raised her eyebrows.

Wing Keung folded his hands in his lap, his expression earnest. "I know you and Ma didn't get along, and that's why you didn't talk to her after you left."

Frankie scoffed. "*Didn't get along?* She told me I was a disgrace to the family. She told me I was a disappointment and that she couldn't bear to have me in her house."

Wing Keung held up a placating hand. "I know."

This was dangerous territory. She and Wing Keung had never discussed this in full before. She had a myriad of feelings involved in what had happened, and she suspected that he didn't want to step on her toes, which was perfectly fine with her.

Wing Keung continued, "She changed over the years, Frankie. I know you don't believe me, but she did. I want you to know that, to think about that while you go through the house. She didn't hate you."

Frankie furrowed her brows. How could her mother not have hated her for all those years? She never called, she never sent a postcard or a letter. She never invited Frankie back home. As far as Frankie was concerned, she had essentially been an orphan since she was twenty-three years old. Her father had left them when she was six, never to be heard from again, and her mother had disowned her.

Wing Keung leaned forward, his hands on the table now. He tilted his head down, looking at Frankie from under his bushy eyebrows. The intensity of his gaze made her squirm—she didn't do *emotions* with him, and there were too many of them in her brother's eyes. "People change," he said, his voice steady. "I changed. When you first came out to me, I said things I regret. But look at us now." He gestured at the two of them sitting across from each other.

Frankie's face was flushed, and she leaned back in her chair, focusing on her breathing. "You are not Ma," she said as calmly as she could. "You've always been more open-minded, more understanding. She was always so rigid. I understand why, but that doesn't make it okay." Even as a teen, Frankie had understood how Ma struggled to balance her traditions with being as *Canadian* as possible. She wanted their family to fit in with the locals, but she wanted them to know their roots too. Frankie had often felt like her mother had tried to force her to live in two different worlds, neither of which she fully belonged in. "What she said to me was not okay. What she *did* was not okay."

Wing Keung nodded slowly. "You're right. It was not okay. But I'm telling you that she changed. Haven't you changed, Frankie?"

He had a point. She was not even close to the same person she had been at twenty-three. A lot could happen in fifty years, and it did. But in her mind, Ma had been static and unchanging, always standing in the kitchen, yelling at Frankie with tears in her eyes, pointing at the front door.

"You don't have to love her, Frankie," Wing Keung said. "I would never ask that of you. But if you could forgive her . . . I know she wanted that. She may not have spoken to you, but I know she wanted to. Can you try to see her for who she truly was?"

Frankie closed her eyes and breathed in the sweet smell of maple syrup and the nutty aroma of her coffee. She opened her eyes and looked at her brother, at the wrinkles between his eyebrows, his wide nose that matched hers, his slightly downturned mouth. "I will try," she said.

He straightened up and grinned. "Good." He picked up his toast again and took a bite, seeming to enjoy it much more now than when he'd started eating. She shook her head, always in awe of her brother's optimism. "So, have you talked to Dylan yet?" he asked between bites.

Frankie frowned. Why was he asking her that? "Not really. Should I?"

It had bothered her that Dylan and Wing Keung had become

so close in her absence. In some ways, it was like Dylan had taken Frankie's place in her family—having dinners with them, celebrating holidays with them. She had to hear about it all from Wing Keung, although he never rubbed it in her face like he could have.

He shrugged. "This is the first time you've seen each other in fifty years. It's an opportunity for you two to reconnect." He was conveniently avoiding eye contact with her, and his tone when he said *reconnect* was decidedly suggestive.

Frankie just about choked on her coffee. "Wh-what?"

Wing Keung shrugged again. "I may be foolish sometimes, but I'm not completely unaware of what goes on around me. I know you liked her as more than a friend, and—although she never said this explicitly—I think that's part of the reason she got divorced." He paused, raising an eyebrow at her. "She's been upset for years at the way you left. I can't talk about you around her without her shutting down. So . . . if you want to apologize, this is your chance."

The waiter came by to refill their water glasses, and Frankie was immensely grateful that she didn't have to respond right away. "I'll think about it," she said once the waiter was gone again, more to end the topic than because she planned to ponder the subject. Of course she felt remorse for leaving Dylan the way she did, even though she didn't regret leaving town. But she was still trying to grasp that her brother knew how she had felt about Dylan. And that he thought Dylan had felt similarly.

"Good," Wing Keung said. "Is it alright if I get another cup of coffee? My energy isn't what it used to be. I don't know how you waited this long to retire."

"Go ahead."

The rest of brunch was relatively painless, and Frankie found herself so preoccupied on the ride back to the Bluebell that she barely noticed her brother's cologne. Before, she had been nervous to see Dylan because she didn't know how she'd react or how

Dylan would react. She'd never even considered that the two of them could be friends again—that seemed like an impossibility.

Frankie had been away for too long, and Dylan was a stranger now. There were fifty years of experiences between them, not to mention how she'd bolted without explaining anything to Dylan.

But Wing Keung's suggestion that they reconnect was like an earworm—she couldn't seem to get it out of her head.

CHAPTER EIGHT

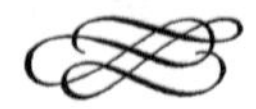

DYLAN

Lorelai answered Dylan's phone call right away and agreed to meet her for lunch at The June Bug. "You're lucky you caught me now instead of this afternoon," she said. "I have a planning meeting with Hijiri and Iris at two."

Hijiri owned Tabletop Time, the board game store on Main Street, and Iris, his wife, was a math teacher at the high school. The two of them went all out for Halloween every year, and this year they had taken on the responsibility of organizing Pumpkin Days with Lorelai. They'd also be hosting the haunted house at the Pumpkin Finale.

"Perfect. I'll see if Evvie, Minnie, and Eleanor can make it. If not, we'll go ahead without them."

"Sounds good. See you then!"

Dylan phoned Evvie first. "I'm sorry, I can't get away from work right now," Evvie said, her frustration apparent in her tone. "Dr. Mel is sick today, and there are a lot of unhappy people coming in." The Juniper Creek Animal Clinic was the only veterinary office in town, and only two doctors worked there. Dylan wouldn't be happy if Darcy or Bingley needed something and couldn't get it, so she could imagine what Evvie was dealing with.

"Okay. I'll keep you posted."

After she hung up with Evvie, she went over to Thistles and Stems. Eleanor was behind the counter, opening spools of ribbon and adding them to the rack on the wall. Plants hung from the ceiling and were displayed on shelves along the side walls in all kinds of eccentric pots.

Eleanor glanced over her shoulder. "Oh, Dylan, good morning! We got more of those book pots you like. One minute." She went through the door to the back room and came back carrying a plant pot that looked like a stack of books. "I made sure to set one aside for you."

"Thanks, Eleanor." Evvie had given her a string of pearls cutting last week that was currently sitting in a cup, and the pot would be perfect for it. Dylan wouldn't have any plants at all if it weren't for Evvie, but her best friend was going through a plant-parent phase and wanted Dylan to experience it with her. It didn't help that Eleanor and Minnie were both florists.

Dylan told Eleanor about lunch as she rang her through and wrapped the pot in tissue paper to prevent it from breaking. "That's perfect," Eleanor said. "Zoey is coming in at eleven, so I can leave her in charge. I don't think we'll be busy today." Weekdays during the fall weren't very busy, which was partially why the town hosted big events on weekends. They needed to keep up revenue all year round in any way they could.

With her new pot safely wrapped and stowed in a bag, Dylan went over to Emily's Garden, which was Minnie's shop. The colors were much more vibrant there than in Thistles and Stems since Minnie sold more flowers than greenery. The sweet smell of the flowers was almost overwhelming. Minnie sat behind the counter, muttering something under her breath as she stared at her computer screen.

"Hello," she called as Dylan came in, the bell over the door tinkling. She looked at her computer again and huffed.

"What's wrong?"

"This program Eleanor has me using is finicky," Minnie said. "I'll admit, it does work better for taking orders. But it's supposed to keep track of numbers and things too, and the spreadsheets don't always work the way I think they should. Anyway, enough about me. What can I do for you?"

After Dylan filled her in on the meeting with Lorelai, Minnie called in an employee to cover for her over lunch, so they were all set. Everyone would be there except for Evvie.

Dylan walked back to the library to get some restocking done before the meeting. She watched the minutes tick by on the clock above the new releases shelf, anxious to pitch her ideas to Lorelai.

There were so many people who used the library every day. There were four caregivers in the children's section right now, reading to their little ones or scrolling on their phones as their kids played at the activity tables. Gwen was helping an older woman apply for jobs on one of the computers, and Olivia from the Bluebell B&B browsed the romance section as she often did. Later that evening, Hugo was hosting Yarn Balls, a group for knitters that Evvie had started a few years ago.

If the library closed, where would these people go? Sure, there were libraries in Abbotsford and the other surrounding towns, but not everyone had the means to get there. The fucking library board knew nothing—they were too far from the action on the ground. If they wanted to close the library, they'd have to go through Dylan to do it.

At noon on the dot, Dylan told Gwen she'd be back in an hour, then she jogged across the street to The June Bug. The weather had cooled off since she'd been out last, and light raindrops speckled her face until she ducked into the diner. Lorelai was already there, sitting in one of the booths with her hands wrapped around a large steaming mug.

Dylan ran her hand through her hair, smoothing out the slight wetness from the rain, and slid into the booth across from Lorelai. "Thanks for meeting with us," she said. "How are you?"

Lorelai smiled without showing her teeth. "I'm alright. Being mayor is not a quiet job, even in a small town." She sighed. "But I love it just the same."

Jamie, the owner of the diner, brought Dylan a pumpkin spice latte just as Minnie and Eleanor came in. "I'll bring you both tea?" she asked as they sat down.

"That'd be lovely, dearie, thank you," Eleanor said.

"Can I have a donut as well, please?" Minnie asked. "I'm feeling peckish."

Jamie nodded, her brown hair swinging over her shoulder as she turned to get their orders. The door opened behind her, and another customer walked in.

Frankie.

Dylan did a double take. Why the fuck was Frankie still in town? She locked eyes with Dylan for a painful second, then she turned and presumably went to sit somewhere. Dylan couldn't see her without craning in her seat, and she didn't want to draw attention from the others.

"So," Lorelai said. "I got the email from the board as well, and Dylan said you have ideas to raise funds for the library. I will do everything in my power to help you. I can't imagine raising Jesse in a town without a library."

Flustered, Dylan said, "Thank you. That means a lot." She glanced over her shoulder but still couldn't see Frankie. It didn't matter where she was, anyway, but the desire to see her was an itch in her brain. She did her best to focus on Lorelai. "It was Minnie's idea to combine fundraising with Pumpkin Days so we could get more attention instead of being ignored in favor of the town's festivities."

"That makes sense," Lorelai said. "So what are you thinking to do?" She reached into a beaded bag on the bench beside her, grumbling under her breath. "I love Jesse, but I do not love crushed Cheerios in my bag." Scowling, she pulled out a notebook and a pen, shaking crumbs off them. "Anyway. I'll run everything past Hijiri and Iris, but I can't imagine they'll be against any of it. If we have the volunteer power and everything is aboveboard, we should be good to go."

Jamie came over with Minnie's donut and Minnie and Eleanor's teas. "What's this I hear about the library?"

Christ, there was no hiding anything from anyone in this town, although it was partially her fault for asking to meet at the diner. Frankie had thrown her off guard, and she couldn't think properly.

Thankfully, Lorelai answered Jamie for her. "We're discussing ways to raise funds for it," she said. "There's a possibility that some libraries in the area might be closing if there isn't enough money by the end of October."

"What?" Jamie pulled a chair over from a table nearby and plunked herself down in it, her eyebrows drawn together. "The library can't close. Tell me what I can do."

Lorelai lowered her voice, causing Dylan, Minnie, and Eleanor to lean in slightly as she spoke. "Well, first of all, we need to keep calm about it. The last thing we need is town hysteria or people taking drastic measures against the board. It's likely that more people will be willing to help than we think; we just have to do things right."

A pencil peeked over Jamie's ear from where she always tucked it, and she pulled it out, twirling it between her fingers and nodding.

"You sound like you have experience with this type of thing," Minnie said.

Lorelai sipped her tea then said, "I've been to a lot of rallies. You don't get to be mayor without experience in politics, and politics are messy."

Dylan hadn't been as involved as Evvie had been in rallies and protests, but she knew how much tension could be in a crowd when people truly cared about something.

"Anyway," Lorelai continued, "back to the ideas. Hit me."

Jamie sat up straighter like a student about to learn material for an exam.

As Eleanor began laying out the plans for a 50/50 raffle at the kick-off, Dylan's attention wandered. Frankie was sitting behind her somewhere, and the urge to turn around was overwhelming. What if Frankie was looking at her right now? What if Dylan turned around and they awkwardly made eye contact?

Dylan perked up when Jamie said something about accepting donations through e-transfer. "We can track e-transfers on a spreadsheet," Dylan said. She loved spreadsheets; she had put together a detailed one to keep track of the vendors at the Sunflower Festival, and she had been quite proud of it. She also tracked her reading that way, writing down book length, author name, publish date, genre, and any representation in the books she read. It helped her read more intentionally.

"I know you'll have that covered," Lorelai said, likely thinking of the Sunflower Festival as well. She added another note to her notebook then looked up expectantly. "Alright, what else?"

This next idea was Dylan's, so she pushed the thought of Frankie to the back of her mind. She needed to focus. "The library has always been involved in the scavenger hunt, but what if we increased our participation this year? The gazebo is usually the hub for the hunt, but we could make the library the hub instead to draw people in. We could have food and drinks available, and a portion of the profit could go to the library."

Holding up her pencil like she was raising her hand, Jamie said, "I'd be happy to donate supplies for food, and I can ask the Dawoods if they'd like to contribute pastries from the bakery."

"I like where you're going with this." Lorelai made another note. "So that's the first two weekends of Pumpkin Days. Would you like to do something for the Finale? It's on October 28, so that's cutting it pretty close to the funding deadline."

"Yes," Minnie said. "There's always a market aspect to the Finale, right?"

The back of Dylan's neck prickled, and her thoughts drifted to Frankie once again. She shook her head slightly to clear it, tuning back in to the conversation as Lorelai said, "There's plenty of street parking, so that would work. I love all of this, and I think Hijiri and Iris will too." Her dangling beaded earrings swung as she nodded and scribbled something else on her notepad. "One more thing, though: volunteer power. Who can we recruit?"

Somehow, Dylan had missed the whole conversation about the market. Frankie was getting to her more than she expected. She clenched her jaw and willed herself to keep her eyes on the prize.

"Me, obviously," Dylan said in answer to Lorelai's question. "And Evvie. She's technically head of the Friends of the Library, so she'll probably spearhead everything with me. She said she has a couple of friends in town who can help as well, including Margie Allen."

"And us, of course," Eleanor said, reaching out and grabbing Minnie's hand from across the table. "We'll do whatever we can. I was also thinking we could recruit Kat and Charlie. It would be good to have some young people on our side." Kat was Eleanor's grandchild, and Charlie was their best friend—both were involved in almost everything Eleanor did. It made Dylan jealous sometimes that her grandkids weren't closer.

Minnie nodded. "I'm sure Kat would love to design flyers. And one of the youths could advertise on social media?"

"Hugo can do that," Dylan said. "He manages social media for the library. Maybe he and Kat can work together to make the branding match."

"Speaking of media," Minnie said, tapping a finger on the table, "we should try to get news coverage somehow. The more people who know about this, the better, right?"

"Yes! Brilliant," Eleanor said, planting a loud kiss on the back of Minnie's hand. Minnie cringed—Dylan cringed with her—but she was smiling.

Lorelai looked at her phone. "I need to get going, but it sounds like we have a plan. I'll get back to you all tonight after my meeting, and we can finalize a larger meeting plan for Saturday. Sound good?"

Minnie scooched out of the booth so Lorelai could leave, then sat back down and poured more hot water for her tea.

Jamie stood as well. "I should actually do my job instead of sitting here, but we'll raise the funds," she said, her eyes glinting with determination. She pushed up her sleeves as if to punctuate her point. "Don't worry about it, Dylan. The library won't be closing any time soon."

One side of Dylan's mouth ticked up. "Thanks, Jamie."

As Jamie walked away, Dylan glanced over her shoulder to look for Frankie again.

"Are you okay?" Eleanor asked. "Are you looking for someone?"

Just as Dylan was about to answer, the *someone* she was looking for walked up to their table. "Hi," Frankie said. "I couldn't help but overhear bits of your conversation. Can I help?"

Dear Library Board,

My name is Jamie, and I own The June Bug diner in Juniper Creek, which is right across the street from the library. The diner used to be my house. I converted it into a restaurant after my parents passed away because it was my dream to continue serving this community. My parents loved this town, and they loved the library too. They did everything in their power to bring people together, and I hope you will do the same.

When I was a kid, I used to go to the library almost every single day. I went there to find new books to read and do my homework without my mom hovering over my shoulder. I participated in every summer reading program until I turned nineteen, and I grew to love science fiction because of the books I found through the weekly challenges. Octavia Butler, Jules Verne, H.G. Wells, and Ursula K. Le Guin were my friends growing up, and now I love Becky Chambers, N.K. Jemisin, Martha Wells, and Mary Robinette Kowal too. They've broadened my view of the world and comforted me when I needed them. I don't know if I would have found them without the library.

I've watched the library grow and change to meet the needs of those around it. It has met my needs and continues to bring people together. If it closes, we will lose the glue of this community.

I can't stand the thought of looking across the street from the diner to see something other than the library. It has been there my entire life, and I want it to be there for me and others for the rest of my life too.

Thanks,
Jamie Marlow

CHAPTER NINE

FRANKIE

Frankie knew she should have started at Ma's house already, but she still hadn't mustered the courage to go in. She hadn't even walked past the outside yet, even though it was only one street over from the library and the Bluebell. She had never procrastinated on getting her photos edited and submitted, and she was clearly making up for that now.

One cup of coffee. She could have one cup of coffee, then she would do it.

At least, that's what she told herself until she saw Dylan sitting at a booth with two other women who appeared to be around their age, and one younger woman with her dark hair braided back. The four of them were having what looked to be an intense conversation.

Frankie seated herself, and the waiter from the other night brought her a cup of coffee and introduced herself as Jamie. As Frankie sipped her drink, Jamie joined Dylan's group, and the discussion seemed to liven up somehow. The women's voices raised slightly in volume, and Frankie caught snatches of conversation, enough to piece together that they were fundraising for something.

The woman with the dark hair left, then Jamie stood up and

said, loud and clear, "Don't worry about it, Dylan. The library won't be closing any time soon."

Something jolted in Frankie's chest. The library was under threat? That building had been her whole world when she was younger; it gave her a safe space to be herself. That's where she had met Dylan and where she had learned about photography. Almost every good memory she had of Juniper Creek happened in the library.

Before she knew what she was doing, she had abandoned her coffee on the table and walked over to where Dylan sat with the two other women. Dylan's eyes widened when she saw Frankie, her mouth falling open.

"Hi," Frankie said. "I couldn't help but overhear bits of your conversation. Can I help?"

Dylan continued to stare at Frankie with her mouth ajar. The woman beside her spoke up, a lilting Scottish accent brightening her words. "Hello. This may sound horribly rude, but who are you? I don't think I've seen you around before. Although, I am relatively new to town." She smiled and raised her eyebrows.

"My name is Frankie," Frankie said. "I'm . . ." Yes, who was she, exactly? Some random woman who used to live here, who had a soft spot for the library.

Dylan cleared her throat. "She's an old friend of mine," she said.

Frankie blinked. The word *friend* made her throat tighten.

"Well, it's lovely to meet you, Frankie," the woman with the long salt-and-pepper hair said. "I'm Eleanor, and this is my girlfriend, Minnie." Eleanor gestured across the table at the third woman, whose cheeks were flushed.

Girlfriend? Finding two women *together* in town—a couple who was out—had been unheard of fifty years ago. It made her heart flutter.

"We can use all the help we can get, right ladies?" Eleanor asked, looking at Minnie and Dylan.

"Yes, of course," Minnie said, smiling at Frankie. Dylan nodded but didn't say anything.

"I need to get back to work, but I'm sure Dylan can give you more details." Eleanor looked to Dylan for confirmation. Dylan nodded and ran a hand through her hair.

The gesture sent a wave of longing through Frankie, so strong she nearly stumbled. Dylan used to run her hand through her hair all the time when she was nervous. It was one of her quirks that Frankie had found so endearing. That she still did it now, in a world that seemed so different, made Frankie's chest ache.

"I should get going as well," Minnie said, standing. "Thank you for organizing this meeting, Dylan. Let us know if we need to meet again this week to prepare for Saturday."

The two of them slipped past Frankie, leaving Dylan sitting in the booth and Frankie standing awkwardly beside the table.

"So," Dylan said, drawing out the word.

"Do you mind if I sit?" Frankie asked.

Dylan shook her head, and Frankie let out a small breath of relief.

"How are you?" she asked as she slid into the booth. "You look good." Even though she looked different than Frankie had imagined through the years, Frankie could see the woman she'd loved in Dylan's laugh lines, in the shape of her face, and in her eyes.

Dylan shrugged. "I'm fine. Well . . . okay, not really. Not right now. But I have been, in general."

A lump formed in Frankie's throat, and she did her best to speak around it. "That's good. Not that you're not alright now, but that you have been . . . doing alright. Wing Keung told me you work at the library?"

"I do." She winced. "Maybe not for much longer, though."

"Why? What's happening?"

As Dylan explained the lack of funding for the library and the plan for raising money, the awkwardness between them lessened.

The library was something they could bond over no matter how long they had been apart.

"What can I do to help?"

Dylan bit her lip. "I'm not sure exactly what you'd like to do, but we have a meeting on Saturday with the Friends of the Library group to talk everything over. You could come to that if you want. We'll be asking for volunteers for the various roles then."

"Okay." That was a good place to start. Frankie willed herself to stay calm; being around Dylan made her heart pound, and what she was asking would mean she'd be around Dylan even more.

Since the library discussion had essentially closed, tension swirled around them once again, filling their silence in a way that made Frankie grimace.

Dylan cleared her throat. "You work for National Geographic now?"

"I did, but I'm retired," Frankie said, grateful that Dylan was continuing the conversation. "Photography was generous to me, and I'm grateful for that. I have a cottage in France now, but Wing Keung asked me to clean out Ma's house before I go. So I'm still here."

"Oh." Dylan cracked her knuckles. Frankie hadn't seen her do that before, reminding her that Dylan wasn't the same person she'd been when she was a teenager. So much had happened since then. So much had changed. "Have you started going through things yet?"

Frankie shook her head. "Not yet."

"Well, let me know if you need help."

Her words seemed sincere. With a jolt, Frankie remembered that Dylan had actually known Ma and probably had feelings attached to the house and Ma's belongings. She frowned and hesitated, then said, "I know that . . . after I left, you became closer with Wing Keung." Dylan clenched her jaw but didn't respond. "Were you . . . were you close to Ma as well?"

Letting out a puff of air, Dylan spun her mug around between her hands. "I don't know if *close* is the right word. I think I knew her well, though. I used to visit your mom for tea, and she invited me over for family dinners. My girls liked her, and my ex-husband did too."

For a second, Frankie's ribs felt as if they were being crushed. Without Dylan's family right in front of her, it was easy for Frankie to forget that Dylan had been married and had three kids. To find out that Ma had known Dylan's kids, though . . . that her kids *liked* Ma . . . the cognitive dissonance threatened to give Frankie a headache. "That's . . . nice," she said, her voice sounding strangled.

"It was," Dylan said. She pushed her mug to the side and clasped her hands together, clearly working up to saying something. "I thought you'd be flying off somewhere as soon as the funeral was over. You know, going to snap photos of hippos in Botswana."

Frankie grinned. "Not quite. Been there, done that."

Dylan smiled, which lit up her face. The two of them were quiet for a moment, then Dylan licked her lips and looked at the table before looking back up at Frankie. She laughed, a short breath of air with no humor in it. "I didn't think I'd ever see you again, and yet here you are. I can't decide how I feel about it."

That was more than fair. Frankie was grappling with her own feelings as well. The last time they saw each other, Dylan had told Frankie that she'd just got engaged. Instead of reacting like a best friend should have—with excitement and expressions of congratulations—she'd turned around and fled. The next day, she left. And she hadn't been back since.

"I understand," Frankie said, her voice low. She looked up, locking eyes with Dylan, needing Dylan to see her honesty. "I'm sorry. I'm sorry I left like that." She shook her head. "I just couldn't—"

Dylan held up a hand. "It's okay. It's in the past. *Fifty years* in the past. I appreciate the apology, though."

Frankie nodded. "You're right, it's in the past." She wasn't entirely sure if she believed that, but it felt better than dwelling on what had happened.

They talked for a few more minutes, Frankie's heart beating hard the entire time. Dylan spoke about her kids and asked about Frankie's cottage, and Frankie told her about the lush countryside and the gorgeously rugged stone wall around her new home.

Dylan looked at her phone screen. "Well, I need to get back to the library. I'll see you on Saturday, right? And let me know if you want help with your mom's house."

"Okay."

With that, Dylan tucked a five-dollar bill under her coffee mug, waved at Frankie, and left.

As far as conversations went, that one hadn't been as bad as Frankie had feared. Dylan didn't seem as upset at her as Wing Keung said she was, and now the two of them would be working together to save the library. And potentially to clean out Ma's house, if Frankie decided she needed Dylan's help; the jury was still out on that one.

Plus, now Frankie had a timeline for when she would get back to France, back to the peace she craved. She'd stay until the end of the month, and she'd book a flight home for after the Pumpkin Finale. That left just under a month to clean out Ma's things.

Dylan's words echoed in her mind: *It's in the past*. Those words sounded ideal, but reality was rarely that easy.

~

The next day, Frankie had breakfast at the Bluebell, caving in to Olivia's insistent comments about her spouse's delicious cooking. She wasn't wrong—Dean did make a decent omelet, and he made Frankie's bacon crispy just like she requested. There was another couple eating in the B&B's cozy dining space as well, dressed in hiking gear, but they left just after her food arrived.

Frankie loitered there while she finished her coffee, still

pushing off going to her mother's house. The afternoon before, she had ordered a large bin to be dropped off in Ma's driveway along with various sizes of boxes—so she could pack up everything that wasn't trash—for donations or for Wing Keung to pick up. All the supplies were ready, but she wasn't.

It didn't make sense that she had so much resistance to cleaning out her mother's things. She may have called Ma by the title of *mother*, but that was all it was: a title. It hadn't meant anything since she left. Even before she left, the word had been fraught with tension for her. Mothers were supposed to be kind and caring, going out of their way to support their children. Frankie's mother had never supported her. No matter how hard Frankie tried to make her happy, Ma had tried to force her to be someone she wasn't time and time again.

So she shouldn't have trouble getting rid of Ma's things, and going into the house she grew up in would be like walking into a stranger's house. At least, that's what she told herself.

Can you try to see her for who she truly was? What had Wing Keung meant by that? Was Ma *truly* the person Margie had described at the funeral, or the person Dylan had described at the diner?

The house key Wing Keung had given her sat in her pocket. She could feel it through the fabric like it was trying to burn a hole in her thigh. She pulled it out, placing it on the table in front of her and staring at it for a few moments.

Sighing, she pocketed the key again and took her empty plate and coffee mug to the window that led to the kitchen where Dean was still cleaning up. "Thank you for breakfast," she said.

He looked up from doing the dishes, his long blond hair pulled off his face with a blue bandanna that matched the walls. "No worries. Tomorrow you gotta try it with the peppers I told you about."

"Maybe," Frankie said, smiling.

He winked at her as he grabbed her dishes.

The sky was overcast when Frankie walked to Ma's house, a

brisk wind tugging her open jacket back below the strap of her satchel. It was only a five-minute walk, but it felt shorter, over before Frankie could properly gather her thoughts. Maybe that was a good thing.

There it was. The house she had lived in with her mother for over a decade. Wing Keung had lived there too when she was younger, but he had moved out and gone to work in Vancouver when he turned nineteen. When he came back, he had dropped his English name, bought his own place, and married Shirley; they had moved back to Vancouver after Wai Lun was born.

Frankie had stayed at home to help Ma with the house and the salon. She also had a part-time job at a café on Main Street that no longer existed. When she looked for it earlier, there was a flower shop in its place. Dylan had gotten a job at the café too so they could spend more time together.

Ma's house looked pretty much how she remembered it, even with the updates Wing Keung had mentioned. A cracked sidewalk led up to three steps and the front door. If you folded the house in half, each side would match perfectly. There was a small window to either side of the dark-green door, and flowers spilled out of the window boxes. Someone must have been taking care of the garden because there was no way everything could be flourishing like that after Ma's four-month stay in the hospital.

The siding was a sickly green color, especially in comparison to the white and brown siding on the neighboring houses. Just as Frankie was wondering what pushed Ma to pick that color siding, rain began pelting down on her. There was no warning; one second it was windy but dry, and the next it was as if she'd stepped straight into a shower on full blast.

That was her cue to go inside.

She ran up the walkway, careful to jump over the crack in the pavement, and fumbled to get the key out of her pocket. The overhang at the front of the roof did little to keep her dry. The key slid smoothly into the lock, and she pushed the door open, quickly closing it behind her.

She stood on a gray mat, a low shoe rack against the wall beside her. She wiped the water off her face then switched on the light. It flickered twice before turning on fully.

Frankie stood in the doorway of her childhood home, listening to the rain pounding on the roof. She thought that being here again would make her feel something, but it was just a house. She slipped her shoes and jacket off, hanging the latter on a coatrack slightly farther in.

She stepped into the living room, the carpet soft under her toes, and that's when it hit her: the smell of Ma's rose perfume and earthy incense. Her feet rooted to the floor and she swayed, reaching out to steady herself on the back of a chair.

Memories flew through her mind like the smell of this room had blown up a dam waiting to burst. She and Wing Keung dancing to "The Twist" in the kitchen while Ma was at work. Sitting at the dining table, watching Ma sew a zipper onto a skirt. Making xia jiao with Ma in the kitchen, her stomach growling as she pinched the edges of the dumplings closed. Going to a plant nursery with Ma and coming back to put together the window boxes, relishing the feeling of dirt under her nails.

Another memory surfaced, framed with joy, hazy at first then even stronger than the others: Dylan sitting on the same couch that was pushed against the wall, Frankie beside her. They had been whispering to each other, something about planning their birthday parties.

Frankie collapsed into the chair she'd been holding on to, her knees giving out.

CHAPTER TEN

DYLAN

The spreadsheet from the Sunflower Festival was still up-to-date since the event had been just over a month ago. Dylan went through to double check the vendor emails and websites, and everything looked accurate. That was where she would start to invite people to grab a spot for the market.

Lorelai had emailed her the night before saying that the meeting with Hijiri and Iris had gone well. Both were on board for all the fundraising ideas, and the town council had approved the expansion of the market into the library parking lot. Now they just needed to get volunteers and execute everything. The first event was on October 14, so they had over a week to prepare and plan.

Raising awareness and advertising the events was essential, so Eleanor was going to speak to Kat right away about designing flyers for the various activities. Hugo assured Dylan that he'd have graphics made and posted on social media as soon as he and Kat came up with a brand scheme, and Evvie was coming to the library in the afternoon to help decorate more.

"We already have decorations," Dylan had said to Evvie on the phone.

"I know," she replied, "but this year it's important that we really make an impression. A sign on your office door and paper leaves on the community board are not enough. It's like a cake with no icing. We need to add icing and sprinkles."

Gwen was planning extra fall activities to draw in more library patrons, so Dylan decided to contact vendors for the market. The more people selling goods, the more money the library would make.

She had just started making a form for potential vendors to fill out when someone knocked on her office door. "What's up?" she said without looking away from the email she was typing.

"Can I talk to you?"

It took a moment for Dylan to recognize who it was—she had been expecting Gwen's gentle soprano or Hugo's gruff baritone, not Frankie's smooth alto.

When Dylan snapped her gaze to the doorway, Frankie still had her fist raised as if she intended to knock again. Her hair was wet, strands of it sticking to her cheeks, and her eyes looked a bit red.

Dylan frowned. "Are you okay?"

Frankie dropped her arm, strangling the strap of her satchel again like she'd been doing when Dylan saw her at the funeral. "I went to Ma's. It . . . it didn't go well."

"What happened?" Dylan sat up straighter and swiveled her chair so she was facing Frankie.

"I had been putting it off." Frankie wiped a droplet of water sliding down her forehead. "I finally got myself there this morning, thinking maybe it wouldn't be so bad. But the smell . . . The house smells like her perfume." She paused, her lower lip trembling slightly. "I couldn't do it," she whispered.

Dylan stood up, her instincts pushing her to wrap Frankie in a hug. But they weren't close like that—not anymore. She lowered her arms, which she had raised halfway, and flexed her hands, feeling at a loss. Seeing Frankie in pain awakened something in her that she thought she'd never feel again. She thought her feelings for Frankie had faded, especially since she'd never expected the opportunity to act on them. "What can I do?" she asked.

Frankie rocked back on her heels. "I know you said you'd help clean out the house, but I was hoping to do it by myself. You've got the library to worry about, and—"

"It's okay. What do you need me to do?" In that moment, it was as if Frankie and Dylan were still teenagers—before Frankie left and everything changed. Dylan would do anything to help her.

"Would you come to the house with me?"

Going to Ms. Wong's house *with Frankie* would be a trip through the past she had never planned to make. But Frankie was standing in her doorway, looking for all the world like she was going to burst into tears. Plus, Dylan was a librarian—wasn't it her job to help people?

"Of course I will," Dylan said. "Do you want to go today? I'm off work at five. Or we can go on Friday? I've got the whole day off."

Frankie sagged against the door as if asking for Dylan's help had taken something out of her. "I'm not sure when I'll be ready to go back in. Can we play it by ear?"

"Of course." Dylan wanted to do more for her but couldn't think of anything besides handing her a tissue from the box on her desk.

Frankie took the tissue and straightened up. "Thanks." She wiped her nose, sniffled, and looked down at her wet clothes. "I'm going to go change into something dry," she said with a laugh.

"Good idea."

Frankie nodded and lifted a hand in farewell. Dylan waited until she'd gone before she sat down again. She was going to help her ex–best friend, who'd left fifty years ago without a word, clean out her mother's house. Her life was turning into a drama.

~

"So, you're going to help her?" Evvie asked, punching holes through red, yellow, and orange paper leaves so she could string them together.

"Of course," Dylan said, handing her another leaf. "What was I supposed to say? 'No, I won't help you. Grieve by yourself. Have fun!' I don't hate her, Ev."

Evvie scoffed. "I was just curious. I think it's nice of you to connect with her again. It sounds like the two of you didn't really leave on a good note the last time you saw each other."

Dylan huffed out a laugh. "You can say that again. I had just told her I was engaged and then . . . she left. Right after I told her, she turned and ran off, then I went to her house the next day to see her, and she was gone. Ms. Wong wouldn't tell me what happened, either. Just that Frankie left."

It still hurt to think about that day. Dylan had been so excited to get married, but her excitement had been overwritten by Frankie's abrupt absence. Over the years, she had reflected on it, and she concluded that it must have been her fault. Getting engaged had hurt Frankie, had pushed her away.

Shortly after her forty-first birthday, Dylan had been reading through her journals from her teenage years, and that's when everything started to make sense. It baffled her that she hadn't seen it before—how she and Frankie had truly felt about each other. She had written about Frankie as one would write about a lover, waxing poetic about Frankie's eyes and her smell, about how she made Dylan feel. One sentence had stood out to her: *I feel like I'm the most myself around her.*

Thank fuck Evvie had been there for her; Dylan didn't know how she would have handled that revelation without her best friend.

Too nervous to reach out to Frankie, she'd confronted Wing Keung about Frankie's feelings, and after some prodding, he'd divulged that Frankie was, in fact, gay.

If Frankie had felt about her the same way Dylan had felt about Frankie . . . Well, it still hurt that she had left without a word, but Dylan understood it better after that moment. If their roles had been reversed, Dylan wouldn't have been happy either.

Evvie paused in her work, her eyes teary as she looked at Dylan. "I'm so sorry. That must have been really hard."

Dylan shrugged and set down the scissors she'd been using to cut out the leaves. "I came to terms with it. It's not like the pain suddenly went away, but it stung less, over time. Are you done with those?"

"Oh, no, sorry." Evvie strung a few more leaves onto the twine then handed one end to Dylan. She wiped her eyes. "I was thinking we could put this along the front desk. So, you're not still upset with her?"

Leave it to Evvie to bring the conversation back around. "I'm not upset. Not anymore." At least, that's what she'd been telling herself for years—while ignoring the painful jolt that went through her chest every time she thought about Frankie.

Her feelings were even more muddled now. Since she'd seen Frankie at the diner, she'd felt something she couldn't name.

Evvie slid the last leaf onto the twine. "Done."

Dylan held up her end. "You know the kids are going to rip this down right away, right?"

"I'm optimistic," Evvie said.

After they put up the leaf banner, Evvie dug out Halloween decals from the bags she had brought in. "For the windows," she said when Dylan quirked an eyebrow at her.

"Can I help?" piped a voice from behind them. It was Ben.

"Are you done your schoolwork for the day?" Dylan asked him. Ben was homeschooled, and Penny, his mother, often brought him to work at the library because he focused better there than at home. The library also had all kinds of resources he could use, and an endless supply of books.

"Yep," he said, bouncing on his toes. "You can ask Mom if you don't believe me. She's looking for books about volcanoes."

"Fine. Then yes, you can help."

He pumped his fist in the air in victory. “Can I put up the bats?”

“Sure.” Evvie smiled and handed him a small stack of bats that would no doubt be crookedly placed all over the windows in the next few minutes.

The two of them stood and watched Ben for a moment before heading over to help. “What will Penny do if the library closes?” Dylan said softly. “She comes in here at least three days a week. And she doesn’t have a car.”

Evvie reached out and grabbed Dylan’s hand, squeezing it once. “It’s not going to close,” she said. “Ben will keep showing up and spouting random facts about things until he’s old enough to think it’s not cool.”

Dylan smiled. “After lunch, he told me that cockroaches won’t die right away if you cut their heads off because their brains are in their body. They’ll die of starvation because they can’t eat.”

“That’s disgusting,” Evvie said, her nose wrinkled.

Dylan nodded and looked fondly at Ben. “Yes, it is.”

Hello library leaders,

I am Ben, and I am eight years old. My mom takes me to the library to learn stuff. These are some of my favorite facts:

- Erupting volcanoes can be so loud that they break windows and make people deaf!!
- There's a type of ant that can live for thirty years!
- Echidnas have touch sensors on their noses that can detect electricity!!
- Venus doesn't have any moons!
- Mangoes come in over five hundred varieties!
- My mom says aliens don't exist, but NASA is still looking for them!!

If the library closes, I won't be able to find facts as easily. I need it to stay open so I can research stuff and so my mom can keep teaching me.

I hope you enjoyed these facts. Keep the library open, and I will send you more!

From,
Ben

CHAPTER ELEVEN

FRANKIE

The next morning, Frankie woke up with a ball of anxiety in her chest at the thought of cleaning out Ma's house with Dylan. In the moment, she hadn't been thinking coherently enough to know why she was running to Dylan of all people, but the more she thought about it, the more it made sense. Dylan had grown up with her and had spent hours with her in that house. It felt appropriate to ask her. Plus, she had offered to help.

They were going to get to know each other all over again, and it was exciting but terrifying at the same time.

Olivia was reading when Frankie went down for breakfast—another romance, judging from the scantily clad heroine on the cover and the man with gleaming muscles who held her close. A library sticker glinted on the book's spine.

"I'm going to try the spicy omelet today," Frankie said in greeting.

Olivia looked up, her face slightly pinker than usual. "Oh, Dean will be happy. He's always trying to get guests to try it, but not many are brave enough. I hope you enjoy it! Maybe have a glass of water handy just in case."

"Alright, I will."

The omelet was spicy, but Frankie had eaten food with much more bite in her life. One of her photographer friends in South Korea had taken her for buldak, also known as fire chicken, and she was sure her taste buds were permanently scarred from that experience.

After finishing her coffee, Frankie went back to her room to grab her camera. She needed to clear her head, and taking photos was the perfect way to do it. It wouldn't hurt to get to know Juniper Creek a bit again, either, since she would be staying here for a few more weeks.

People often thought you had to travel far outside of cities to photograph wildlife, but there was plenty to see in urban areas as well if you had an eye for it. The weather here was still warm, which helped. Frankie had a thin sweater on over her T-shirt, and she suspected she'd need to take it off this afternoon.

Her plan was to go to the pond on the other side of the park. A walking path ringed the body of water, most of the pathway shadowed in bushes and trees. The trees had always inspired awe in Frankie; they were the biggest beings she'd ever seen, towering so high above her that she couldn't see the tops. She'd seen other breathtaking natural structures since she'd lived in Juniper Creek, but she'd always had a soft spot for trees.

Benches were spaced along the path for people to take breaks or sit and think for a while. Frankie and Dylan used to go for walks there all the time, and Frankie brought her camera on most of those days. There were all kinds of animals to take pictures of: birds, fish, ducks, turtles, and beavers. Insects, too, and otters if she was lucky.

The library was on the way to the pond, and Frankie walked past the doors then backtracked. It wouldn't do any harm to stop in, just to look around.

She knew Dylan would be there, but she'd be working, not paying attention to Frankie. Frankie told herself she was happy about that, and yet something in her longed for Dylan's attention.

"Good morning," a mousy-haired librarian said when Frankie walked through the sliding doors. Her name tag read "Gwen."

Frankie gave her a wave. This was the first time she had the mental capacity to really look around at everything. When she came in the day before, she'd been so distraught that another librarian named Hugo had practically walked her straight to Dylan's office door.

Despite her lack of observation skills the last time she was here, Frankie noticed the library had become more fall themed. Strings of colorful leaves hung from the front desk and from the new releases shelves, Halloween decals adorned the windows, and tiny decorative pumpkins sat on the checkout desks. There was also a display of fall books front and center with a sleeve of Pumpkin Days pamphlets. Frankie grabbed one and tucked it into her bag.

Weaving around the comfy chairs set in circles around low coffee tables, Frankie approached the "Recommended" shelves on the opposite side of the library. The shelves were labeled "Places," "People," and "Prose." Because Frankie had traveled so much, she didn't have an extensive book collection. One of her favorite things to do was go into a bookshop or a library and pick up whatever called to her in that moment. She often found beautiful and haunting books that way, stories that lingered in her mind like a strong flavor lingered on your tongue. Since she couldn't keep them, she passed them on and hoped other readers would love them as much as she did. *Pride and Prejudice* was the one book she couldn't let go of.

"This one is good," said a woman beside her. She had an accent that Frankie couldn't quite place—Filipino, maybe? She pointed to a book in the "People" section titled *From the Ashes* by Jesse Thistle. "It's a memoir. I'm new to Canada, and I've been reading many books to learn about this place."

Frankie picked up the book as the woman continued browsing. "Thank you," she said, flipping it over to read the description. It sounded like something she would enjoy—a true story, a reflection of place and belonging, and a character study of sorts—but she wasn't sure if she could check out books since she didn't live in the area.

She brought it over to the desk. "Hi," she said. The mousy librarian—Gwen—looked up at her from the computer. "I don't have a library card, but I was wondering if there's a way for visitors to check out books?"

Gwen didn't even blink at the question; she probably heard it all the time from tourists coming through town. "Do you live in the Fraser Valley at all? We've got twenty-five different libraries in our system, so you can take out a book if you belong to one of those."

She'd suspected as much. "No, but that's okay. Thank you anyway." She was turning to leave when Dylan strode behind the desk and slid *From the Ashes* out from under Frankie's hand.

"You can check it out under my name," she said. "Since you'll be here until the end of the month, right?" Dylan's hair stuck up like she'd been running her hands through it again, and it took a second for Frankie to absorb what she'd said.

"Yes. Thank you." She swallowed hard.

"I'll let you handle it, then," Gwen said. "I'm going to restock the ukuleles. They are oddly popular lately."

"Sounds good," Dylan said, her eyes on the computer screen. "Here you go." She held out the book to Frankie. "This one is worth reading. The author recently had a daughter, and you can follow their family online if you're into that kind of thing."

Frankie picked up the book and held it to her chest. "You rent out ukuleles?"

Dylan snorted. "Sounds ridiculous, I know. We've been trying to stock non-traditional things to increase library usage. It's been working, and it has been surprisingly fun. We have bird-watching kits, which see a ton of use in the spring and summer, and we've also had telescopes in. Rubik's Cubes are big with teenagers for some reason."

"That's wonderful." Frankie wasn't exaggerating—she would

have loved to rent out some of those things when she was a kid. Her mother had been particular about her toys and hobbies, pushing her toward domestic work and away from what she considered more masculine activities. When Frankie got her first camera—which hadn't been easy—she hid it for months because she had been scared that Ma would take it away. She had let Frankie keep it when she eventually found it, but she didn't encourage Frankie's hobby any more than she encouraged Wing Keung playing poker with his friends.

"You brought your camera?" Dylan asked, gesturing with her chin toward the big black camera hanging from a strap around Frankie's neck.

Frankie raised her eyebrows. "I've been a professional photographer for over three decades. You think I'd travel without my camera?"

The expression Dylan gave her was almost a smirk. "Good point. I've seen your work—it's fantastic." She seemed to realize what she said, and her gaze flicked down to the table.

"You've seen my work?" The fluttering in Frankie's chest grew stronger.

Dylan looked back up at her, the tips of her ears bright red. "I've been known to read a *National Geographic* magazine every once in a while. I'm a librarian, remember?"

"Yes." An odd feeling of warmth spread through Frankie's body. Over the years, she had often wondered if Dylan would see her photos and think of her. She wanted to ask Dylan what she thought in more depth. Did she like Frankie's subject choices? Her color palettes? What about the tenderness and vulnerability she tried to capture?

"Anyway, I need to get other stuff done. See you around?"

I hope so. "Sure." She watched Dylan walk to her office and close the door.

Frankie left the library and crossed the street toward the pond.

The technology in the library had changed and it offered more services now, but it seemed like people were at home there as much as they'd been when Frankie was growing up. She used to go there almost every day after school to do her homework or find a new book to read, and Dylan often went with her.

The fresh air outside helped her relax, and her heart lifted at the first flicker of movement out on the water. It was an eared grebe swimming gently through the lily pads, its bright red eye almost glaring against the woodland colors surrounding it. Frankie moved in closer to the pond and crouched down, doing her best not to make any noise. The grebe probably wouldn't be bothered even if she did break a few twigs; many people walked this path daily.

She snapped a few photos, catching the water droplets on the grebe's back and the flared yellow feathers fanning out around its eye. Satisfied, she stood and continued her walk.

She photographed three chickadees and a woodpecker as she walked, each flicker of the shutter grounding her more. The events of the past few days didn't matter at all as she breathed out and depressed the shutter release.

On the far side of the pond, she came across a little wooden gazebo sheltering a bench where a woman sat, a sunhat on her head. The gazebo provided a fantastic view of the water. Frankie walked along the path toward the gazebo's railing. When she reached the front, the woman turned to her. "Margie! Good morning."

"Frankie, hi! It's nice to see you out around town again. Taking photos?" She gestured to Frankie's camera.

"Yes. It helps clear my head."

Margie nodded sagely. "I imagine you need that after this weekend. How are you doing?"

"I'm as good as I can be, I think," Frankie said over her shoulder as she moved to the gazebo railing. A log peeked up over the waterline not far away, and a frog sat almost motionless on it. Frankie adjusted her settings so the camera could focus better, then she took the photo.

"Do you mind if I sit for a bit?" she said, gesturing to the bench beside Margie.

"Not at all. I'm glad you're here, actually. I was going to find you later at the Bluebell."

"Oh?"

"Yes. Well"—Margie wrung her hands—"I have some news. I haven't told you yet because it didn't feel right to say this over the phone. And then I couldn't bring myself to tell you when you arrived on Saturday. You had just got off the plane, and it was right before the funeral, and I didn't want to make everything about me."

Frankie shifted so she faced her friend. "Is everything alright?"

Margie nodded. "It's more than alright, really." She paused. "You see . . . I found someone."

"You . . . found someone?"

Clearing her throat, Margie continued, "I met someone. A few months ago."

Frankie's jaw dropped. "Margie! You're dating someone? That's fantastic!" Margie had struggled when her husband passed away three years earlier, and that was the only time in the past five decades that Frankie had truly considered going back to Juniper Creek. It was hard to watch Margie suffering from so far away, to feel so helpless. "Tell me all about him."

Margie's face took on a pink tinge and she breathed in deeply. "*Her* name is Gem."

Everything seemed to slow down, and then Frankie was grinning. She grabbed Margie's hands. "*Her* name? You're with a woman?" Not in a million years would Frankie have seen this coming. "Good for you, Marge. Tell me all about this *Gem*."

The tinge of pink had spread down Margie's neck now, and she smiled. "We met one day in April. At this very bench, actually."

Frankie leaned back. "Tell me everything." Over the next hour, she listened to Margie's story, grinning the entire time and thinking of Wing Keung's argument that people could change.

Margie had certainly changed, and Frankie was over the moon for her.

~

FRANKIE SPENT the rest of the afternoon taking photos, her mind blissfully empty of thoughts of Dylan or Ma. When she looked through the camera, the world narrowed to what she could see and feel in that moment. Nothing else mattered.

She pushed off the pain in her neck from the camera weight for as long as she could before heading back to the Bluebell right before dinner, thinking about Margie and her new flame. The bright blue wallpaper in her room seemed extra cheerful when she dropped off her bag and her camera, and even not being able to carry her camera for as long as she used to didn't spoil her mood.

She joined the B&B's three other guests in the small dining room for dinner. Dean had put together a curry dish, and the smell of it made Frankie's mouth water. He also baked little apple tarts for dessert.

Instead of going upstairs straight after dinner like she'd been doing every day so far, Frankie made herself comfortable in the lobby and read *From the Ashes* as Olivia read her romance novel and Dean brought them both tea.

Even with the awkwardness of interacting with Dylan, Juniper Creek was starting to seem like an acceptable place to be for a month. As far as Frankie knew, there were at least two not-straight couples out in the town now, both older, which meant that the chances of younger queer people being there too were high. And the library had shifted with time as well, bringing in new technology and catering to the tastes of its patrons.

The town was still small and had its flaws, but maybe it had changed more than she thought. It didn't seem like the worst place to stay for the next month. But only for a month. She had no intentions of staying longer than that.

CHAPTER TWELVE

DYLAN

More people showed up to the Friends of the Library meeting on Saturday than Dylan had expected, making the small meeting room feel pleasantly crowded. Her heart soared to see so many townspeople from all different walks of life willing to help with fundraising and organizing to keep the library open, especially on Thanksgiving weekend when many people went out of town or spent the weekend with their families. It was the same cozy feeling she got when she read books with the found-family trope—the library patrons were her found family.

Minnie and Eleanor were there, of course, as was Evvie since she was chair of the Friends group. She sported her rainbow scarf over a loud patchwork dress, and she was talking to two of her friends from her queer seniors' group who had come to support the library. Dylan knew Margie because she lived in town, but the other woman was unfamiliar to her. Evvie had introduced her as Gem, if Dylan remembered correctly.

She recognized most of the other people as well. Hijiri and Iris were there, although they had to be since the library fundraising was going hand in hand with Pumpkin Days. Hijiri wore a graphic T-shirt referencing what Dylan suspected was a meme, and Iris wore dark jeans with a beautiful wraparound blouse. Kat and Charlie were sitting with Charlie's older sister—who worked with Minnie at Emily's Garden—and a few of their friends from high school. Their English teacher, Mr. Flores, was there too with two other teachers. Vera, Kat's mom, sat with her head close to Jamie's; the two of them had been attached at the hip for as long as Dylan could remember. Olivia and her husband, Dean, had closed the Bluebell for a couple of hours so they could make the meeting, and Leah had done the same with Yellow Brick Books. A few other library patrons were there as well.

Then there was Frankie. She had walked in a few minutes ago and waved at Dylan before going to sit beside Margie. Dylan's spirits had lifted at that wave. After fifty years without seeing Frankie around town, it felt right to have her back and involved with fundraising. She wasn't about to get too comfortable with the feeling, though, since Frankie was leaving in less than a month.

Evvie moved to the front of the room and clapped her hands. "Hello, everyone," she said, projecting her voice impressively. "Thank you, all, for coming to this meeting. We organized this last minute and I know it's a long weekend, so I'm pleased by how many people showed up. As we explained in the email, we're going to be fundraising at the Pumpkin Days festivities to keep the library open. We have different plans for each weekend . . ."

After Evvie ran through each of the different fundraising activities, she asked for volunteers for various roles. Frankie volunteered to organize the market, and since Dylan had the spreadsheets for the vendors and had already sent a few emails, it meant the two of them would be working together. Her stomach flipped at the thought.

Everything else was covered within half an hour.

Mr. Flores cleared his throat. "Before we wrap up, can I pitch an idea? My students had a brainstorming session the other day and came up with it." He nodded at Kat, Charlie, and their friends with a smile.

"Of course," Evvie said. "We're all ears."

"We were thinking," Mr. Flores continued, "that it might be helpful to collect letters from library users in which they write about why they love the library. We know this is about funding more than anything, but sending our stories to the board might give us a boost. Patrons could email their letters to me, or to the library, and we could send them all in a package before the end of the month. We could call them Letters From a Friend."

Warmth spread through Dylan's chest at the idea. She'd love to read those letters—to see why people loved the library in their own words. "I'd be happy to collect those," she said. "People can send them to the library email or bring them in if they're handwritten."

"That's a fantastic idea," Evvie said, her eyes sparkling. Many others nodded and murmured their agreement.

After a few closing remarks, Evvie handed out information packets to the volunteers and the meeting was adjourned. All they had to do now was execute their plans.

It was moments like this that gave Dylan hope. If this many people were working toward saving the library, there's no way they'd come short of their fundraising goal.

Gwen brought in trays of cookies, and the people who hadn't run back to their businesses stayed to mingle. Including Frankie.

"Hello," she said quietly, coming over to Dylan when there was a break in the crowd. She had a chocolate chip cookie on a napkin in her hand. "It seems like you had a good turnout."

"I think so." Warmth had spread through Dylan's chest during the meeting and was still there, glowing. It had nothing to do with Frankie. Absolutely nothing.

Evvie bustled over with Gem and Margie in tow. "That went well, I think," she said.

"I'd say so," Gem added. Her fingers were entwined with Margie's, umber brown clasped with rosy white. "This library isn't going anywhere."

Margie smiled and nodded.

"You must be Frankie," Evvie said, holding out her hand. Although the two of them had seen each other at the funeral, they hadn't been formally introduced.

Frankie wiped her fingers on her napkin and shook Evvie's hand firmly. "I am, yes. Evvie, right?"

"That's me!" She glanced at Dylan. That glance meant something, but Dylan wasn't sure exactly what it was.

"Sorry, I'm bad at introductions," Dylan said. "Frankie, this is Evvie. You already know Margie. And maybe Gem?"

"Yes," Gem said. "Margie introduced us earlier."

Frankie nodded and smiled at Gem.

Margie suppressed a smile. "I'm glad you two got to meet." She turned to Evvie and Dylan. "Thank you for the meeting today," she said, "but we should get going. My grandchildren are coming over today for Thanksgiving, and I want to have dinner ready for them when they get here."

After hugging Frankie, Gem and Margie departed, and Dylan was left standing with Frankie and Evvie.

"When did you meet Margie?" Evvie asked Frankie.

"Oh, I was in the same grade as Margie, so we went to school together. And she worked with Ma at the salon."

"Oh!" Evvie put a hand over her face. "Of course she did. Sorry. I remember now, from the funeral."

Frankie continued, "Gem seems nice."

Evvie beamed at her. "She is. She started an LGBTQ+ seniors' group I'm part of. Margie hasn't joined us yet, but I think she will one day. We meet in Abbotsford every week, if you're interested in joining us."

Dylan had the urge to smack Evvie's arm. Evvie had just revealed—or at least implied—that Dylan had been talking to her about Frankie. Otherwise how would Evvie know that Frankie was queer? Dylan didn't want Frankie knowing that she'd been keeping tabs on her.

"Um, thanks," Frankie said. "I don't really want to put down any roots here, but I appreciate the invitation."

At the reminder that Frankie wasn't really *back*, Dylan swallowed hard.

"Would you like to go for coffee?" Evvie asked Frankie. "The three of us, I mean. Dylan has the rest of the day off, and it might be nice for us to get to know each other. If you're alright with that, Dylan."

What was that supposed to mean? Dylan narrowed her eyes at her best friend, and Evvie widened her own eyes back in a look of genuine curiosity.

"Why wouldn't I be?" Dylan said. She hadn't spoken to Frankie much yet, so she still didn't really know who she was now.

Evvie shrugged one shoulder then turned to Frankie again. "I like to know the people I work with, and I'm grateful that you'll be helping us with the market. I also like to know the people Dylan is friends with."

Dylan bit her lip. She'd have a word with Evvie later. Sure, everything she said was perfectly peachy on the surface, but there was an implication there that Frankie meant something to Dylan.

She did, in some ways. She was an important part of Dylan's past, and Dylan had realized she was gay because of Frankie, but now they were barely friends.

"That sounds nice," Frankie said. "I'm not doing anything else this afternoon."

They walked down Main Street to Dawood Bakery with Evvie and Frankie walking side by side in front of Dylan. The arrangement meant that Dylan couldn't hear everything they were saying, which bothered her. The snippets of conversation she caught seemed to revolve around the library and the town.

"This is a cute bakery," Frankie said as they stepped inside. "I should have come here earlier."

"Where have you been going?" Evvie asked.

"The diner, mostly. And the Bluebell because I'm staying there, and Dean makes tasty food."

"The bakery supplies the diner with pastries," Dylan said, inserting herself into their conversation. "So you might have had their food even if you haven't been here before." She walked up to the counter. The display case was still relatively full of baked goods, which wasn't surprising since it was fall and nothing was happening in town this weekend. During the summer and on festival weekends, the bakery sold out of the best pastries by noon.

Aaliyah was working behind the counter today, and the warm scent of freshly baked cake wafted out of the back room. "I'm sorry I couldn't make the meeting," she said, adjusting her hijab. "Kamran had a dentist appointment in Chilliwack, and I didn't want to close the shop."

Dylan waved a hand. "No problem. We had a good turnout, anyway. You still want a stall for the market?"

"Yes, of course."

Pushing up beside her, Evvie said, "Frankie here will be managing the market setup."

Frankie waved.

"Oh, wonderful," Aaliyah said. "Thank you for handling all of that. Whatever you want today, it's on the house."

Kamran and Aaliyah were always giving away food and drinks for any little thing someone did for them. Dylan thought it was a bad financial decision, but their hospitality seemed to garner loyalty. In a town this small, loyalty could make or break a place. Like the library.

Aaliyah slid open the display case from the back and used tongs to grab what looked like a little pumpkin. "I'm trying these out, if you'd like one. They're pumpkin chai cakes with a chocolate curl."

Evvie moaned and pulled on the ends of her scarf. "That sounds amazing. I want one, please. Can I also get a pumpkin steamed milk?"

They did sound delicious. "Same for me," Dylan said.

Aaliyah nodded and turned her brown eyes on Frankie, one eyebrow elegantly lifted.

"I would like the same, please, but with a coffee," Frankie said.

Once they had their drinks and pastries, they made themselves comfortable at a table by the wall. Dylan ate her cake, letting the other two continue whatever conversation they'd been having before they came in.

"So, what's your favorite place you've ever been?" Evvie asked. She sipped her drink and leaned forward, her elbows on the table. Dylan caught herself leaning forward as well and forced herself to sit with her back pressed against the chair.

Frankie made a humming sound and sat back in her chair as well, both hands wrapped around her mug. "That's a tough question. I've been to a lot of places. I guess . . . I enjoyed going to Hong Kong. My family is from there. I don't know any relatives who still live there, but it was interesting to see where my ancestors came from."

For as long as Dylan had known her, Frankie had barely talked about her family history other than to complain about how traditional her mom was. They had celebrated Lunar New Year and the Mooncake Festival, but Dylan couldn't remember Frankie being very interested in Chinese culture beyond that and the food she ate on a daily basis.

"What made you change your mind about connecting with your roots?" Dylan asked, genuinely curious.

"Honestly, it was my job. National Geographic asked me to go, and I found myself wanting to more than I expected. I'm still not very connected to my roots," Frankie continued. A frown tinged with sadness flashed across her face. "But I got to photograph pink dolphins, civets, and pangolins, which not everyone can say." She sighed and her brow furrowed. "Ma always talked about going to Hong Kong one day." She turned her gaze to Dylan. "Did she ever get there?"

Dylan shook her head, her pumpkin cake suddenly not tasting as good as it had two minutes ago. "No. She talked about it a lot, though."

Frankie nodded and shrugged. She finished off her pumpkin cake, licking a crumb off her lip. Dylan pulled her gaze away from Frankie's mouth, her face flushing.

"Are you doing anything tomorrow?" Evvie asked Frankie.

Frankie raised an eyebrow, her mouth still full.

Evvie continued, "We don't really celebrate Thanksgiving, but Dylan, Eleanor, Minnie, and I have weekly Sunday night dinners. You met Minnie and Eleanor at the diner, I think, and they were at the meeting. You could join us tomorrow, if you'd like. Then you'll have more variety than food from the diner and the Bluebell."

"That's nice of you to offer, but I'm going to my brother's house for dinner with him and his wife."

"Oh. That makes sense," Evvie said. "Well, you'll have to join us another day then."

The thought of Frankie joining them for their weekly dinners made Dylan's heart flutter. It made it seem like Frankie was a normal part of everything, not someone who was just visiting.

"Can I ask you two something?" Frankie said.

"Of course. Ask away," Evvie replied.

"Are you . . . You two seem close. I know it's presumptuous of me to ask, but are you together?"

Evvie laughed and Dylan just about choked on her pumpkin cake. Why did people always think she and Evvie were together? "No," she said, spluttering. The thought of being with Evvie *like that* was ridiculous. They'd been best friends for years, more like siblings than anything.

"You're not the first person to think so," Evvie said, putting her hand lightly on Frankie's arm. "But no, we're just friends."

Was Dylan imagining things, or did Frankie's shoulders relax slightly? Why would she care if Dylan and Evvie *were* together? Was she interested in Evvie? Maybe she wanted to know if Dylan had found someone else, which made Dylan wonder if *Frankie* had found someone else. Wing Keung had never said anything about Frankie's love life besides subtly confirming that Frankie was also gay. Dylan pursed her lips.

She needed to change the subject. "So, Frankie, have you

decided when you'd like to start going through your mom's house? I'm trying to figure out my schedule for next week."

Frankie took another sip of coffee. "Oh, sorry. I suppose I shouldn't leave that open-ended. It's okay if you don't want to help, though. I can ask Margie."

"Hey." Dylan felt defensive suddenly. Why would Frankie think she wouldn't want to help, especially after she said she would? She reached out and put her hand on Frankie's arm, a thin line of electricity sizzling under her palm. "I *want* to help." She wanted to help for Ms. Wong and for Wing Keung, but she had another motivation now as well. This was a chance to get to know Frankie all over again.

"I'll help too, if you need another set of hands," Evvie said. "I work at the animal clinic, but I can come over if I'm not working. And if I'm not doing something for Pumpkin Days or the library." Her brow furrowed.

"You're kind of busy, Ev," Dylan said. This was not the first time Evvie had been overbooked lately. Her job was taking a lot out of her. "Are you sure you don't want to retire?"

Evvie glared at Dylan. "We've already talked about this." Evvie was financially stable enough that she could have retired years ago, but she insisted that she'd have nothing to do if she wasn't working. "I don't have a family like you do," she'd say. "Work is my life."

Dylan shrugged then turned back to Frankie. "I've got Monday and Friday off, as usual, and I could help out after work on the other days."

"Monday would work well," Frankie said. "I keep putting it off, but I need to get it done eventually."

"Okay."

Two more days, and she'd be alone with Frankie.

Frankie opened her satchel and pulled out the welcome packet Evvie had given her at the library. "I noticed something in here about a spreadsheet," she said, and Dylan grinned with pride. "Where can I get that? I'd like to start on this tomorrow if I can."

"I can send it to you. What's your email?" Dylan pulled out her phone so Frankie could put in her info, but Frankie beat her to it with a good old-fashioned notebook and pen from her satchel.

"Here," she said, handing Dylan a strip of paper. Dylan's fingertips tingled where Frankie's fingers brushed hers. "You should have my email too, just in case," she said as she wrote out her email address again for Evvie. "Is the library open tomorrow? I'd love to work there if it's available."

Dylan nodded. "We've got reduced hours, but Hugo will be there. We're closed on Monday."

"I am so looking forward to having Monday off," Evvie said, closing her eyes and sighing. "Leaving early today for the meeting was like trying not to sing during *The Rocky Horror Picture Show.*"

Another comment about retiring jumped to Dylan's mind, but she bit her lip to keep from saying it.

Frankie tilted her head at Evvie. "What do you do at the animal clinic?"

Evvie carried the conversation until they were done with their drinks.

Despite the two of them being so close at one point in their lives, Dylan didn't know how to act anymore around Frankie. There was so much she didn't know about her now.

It didn't make sense that something simmered low in her belly whenever she looked at Frankie. And that the something grew stronger at the thought of the two of them spending time alone together.

Dear members of the Library Board,

The library has always been an important part of my life. My parents used to take me there when I was a kid, and I loved playing with the toys and reading books with my mom. Now my best friend and I go there to work on our homework and to hang out. There are so many different types of people that use the library, and I've learned so much just from talking to people.

It'd be more than a shame if the library closes. We'd be losing a piece of all of us. I hope we can raise enough money to keep it open because I don't want to see that happen.

Sincerely,
Kat Lefebvre

CHAPTER THIRTEEN

FRANKIE

On Sunday, Frankie went to the library as soon as it opened.

Hugo was at the front desk, and he waved at her when she came in. "I'm glad you're helping us with fundraising," he said. A grin spread across his face, revealing a slightly crooked front tooth.

"Of course. This place means a lot to me."

"Me too."

She found a seat at a table with an outlet under it and set up her laptop. While she waited for it to turn on fully, she people watched. An older gentleman was coloring with a little girl—presumably his granddaughter—in the children's section. Something about him looked familiar . . . he had been at the meeting on Saturday. Mr. Flores, maybe? She moved on to someone else so she wouldn't be staring like they were subjects of a photograph. Hugo was now helping someone at the computer. A short, round woman with blond hair pulled back in a bun leaned over a boy working at the table closest to Frankie, and Frankie could hear her explaining a math equation.

It was odd to see so many people of color around town; it was yet another sign that Juniper Creek had changed. In addition to the two library patrons in the room with her, Hijiri—the man running Pumpkin Days with his wife—was Japanese. When Frankie was growing up, her family was one of only three Asian families in town, and she had put up with more than her fair share of comments about her eyes and what she brought to school for lunch. She wondered if kids were still mean like that now.

Finally, her computer loaded and pinged with an email notification, and she was glad for the distraction. When she saw the email, she scoffed. It was yet *another* offer from the movie company who had been trying to buy her cottage from her for months. She turned them down every time, but they kept contacting her with a higher offer.

She deleted the message then threw herself into emailing the vendors according to the information Dylan had sent her.

Dylan herself was nowhere to be found, which was fine. Frankie didn't need to see her for any particular reason.

She took a quick break to run over to the diner for lunch; she'd heard someone at the library talk about how good the burgers were, and they were not exaggerating. "It's my secret sauce," Jamie said to her with a wink when she brought Frankie's plate over. "And before you ask, no, you cannot buy some to take home. I'm possessive." She laughed and Frankie shook her head in amusement.

When she took her seat at the library again, she caught a glimpse of Dylan in her office, head bent over a binder full of papers.

Frankie got down to work, researching more possible vendors for the market since the available space wouldn't be full even if everyone she had already emailed booked a spot. There were tons of small businesses in the Fraser Valley, so she wasn't worried. If worst came to it, she could reach out to businesses in Vancouver too.

Dylan passed by her table a few times as she went about her librarian duties, but she didn't stop to talk. She made eye contact with Frankie once and nodded, but that was it.

Frankie didn't know what she had expected to happen once

the two of them were in proximity again, and it was disarming to see Dylan go about her regular life—a life that Frankie had no part in. If Frankie had stayed, where would each of them be now?

At three, Frankie headed back to the Bluebell. Shirley was picking her up at five-thirty for dinner, and Frankie found herself looking forward to Wing Keung's fried turkey.

~

"CAN YOU PLEASE PASS THE POTATOES?" Wing Keung asked. It was just the three of them for dinner since Wai Lun was still away on business.

Frankie pushed the potatoes over to him.

"Thanks," he said.

"Thank you for making dinner," Frankie said, spreading cranberry sauce on her turkey. "This is the first Canadian Thanksgiving I've celebrated since I moved from Juniper Creek."

"It's not a problem," Wing Keung said. "I love deep frying turkey!"

Shirley laughed and looked at him fondly, then she turned to Frankie. "It's the only thing he enjoys cooking. I cook the rest of the time."

Wing Keung snorted.

"Well, this is delicious," Frankie said, and she wasn't lying. It was the best turkey she'd had in years.

"I'm glad you like it," her brother said, putting a piece of turkey in his mouth and looking rather proud of himself.

"So, Frankie." Shirley dabbed at her mouth with a cloth napkin. "How's the house cleaning going?"

Frankie ducked her head. "I haven't started it. But someone will be helping me, and we're starting for sure tomorrow."

Wing Keung's gaze snapped up to her. "*Someone?*"

"Yes, someone."

"Is that *someone's* name Dylan, by chance?"

"Maybe." She glared at him.

Shirley looked back and forth between them, her brow furrowed. "Okay," she said, drawing out the word. "Well, let us know if we can do anything."

Wing Keung sipped his wine. "As long as it doesn't involve me moving too much."

Scoffing, Shirley glared at her husband. "Don't listen to him. We'll do whatever you need us to do."

Frankie stayed up late that night, going through photos with Shirley. Frankie was in a few of the albums, but most of them showcased her brother's life without her.

"It's good to have you here," Shirley said, setting her hand on Frankie's arm. "We miss you. Your brother won't say so, but I know he's happy to have you around more."

She showed Frankie to the guest room where she'd be spending the night. "Let me know if you need anything. I can drive you back to the Bluebell in the morning."

As Frankie lay in bed, she mulled over Shirley's words. She wouldn't say so either, but she was happy to be around more. Moving from place to place for her job got tiring, and she'd been looking forward to settling down in France. But she hadn't made her cottage a true home yet, leaving most of her worldly possessions in boxes.

This evening with her brother and his wife had reminded her that sometimes, being around family wasn't so bad. Being with them helped her see that settling down was possible, and she looked forward to making the cottage more of a home when she got back to France.

CHAPTER FOURTEEN

DYLAN

They hadn't made plans on where to meet on Monday or at what time, so Dylan emailed Frankie on Sunday and they decided to meet in front of Ms. Wong's house at 11:00 a.m. She could have asked Frankie about the time when she saw her at the library, but she'd been too focused on finishing up the weekend tasks. No matter how aware she was of Frankie—which seemed to be way too fucking aware—she would not let herself get distracted.

Dylan took Darcy and Bingley for a walk around the pond first thing on Monday. Once the dogs were settled, she walked over to Ms. Wong's house. The last time she'd been there had been after Wing Keung called her to let her know about Ms. Wong's passing. Dylan had cleaned out the fridge, knowing it was one of those tasks that needed to be dealt with sooner rather than later.

As Dylan approached the house, she spotted Frankie rocking back and forth on her heels on the sidewalk out front. She stared at her childhood home like it might reveal its secrets to her if she looked at it long enough. A large dark blue bin sat in the driveway, which Frankie had probably ordered to aid with cleaning out the house.

The sound of Dylan's footsteps must have signaled her approach—Frankie looked up and gave her a small wave, her other hand on her satchel strap.

"Good morning," Frankie said, glancing at the house then back to Dylan. "I really appreciate you being here."

"No problem." When Frankie didn't reply, Dylan asked, "Are you ready?"

Frankie took a deep breath. "As I'll ever be."

As they walked up the path to the front door, Dylan stayed back a couple of feet so she wouldn't crowd Frankie. Before she went inside, Frankie pushed her shoulders back and tilted her chin up. Dylan recognized how she donned her mental armor; she'd done the exact same thing when she was younger.

When Dylan stepped into the house, Frankie had already flicked the light on. It smelled a bit musty, but as they moved farther into the place, Dylan smelled the rose perfume and the lingering woodiness of incense. Stacks of unfolded boxes leaned against the wall, which hadn't been there before. Frankie let Dylan pass her on their way into the living room. "Are you okay?" Dylan asked, turning back to look at her.

Her expression was placid, put together. Her face was surprisingly smooth for her age—especially compared to Dylan's—and Dylan found herself wanting to run her fingers over Frankie's cheeks, over her forehead, over her lips.

"I'm alright," Frankie said, barely moving her mouth. If Dylan couldn't see her chest moving, she would think Frankie wasn't breathing.

"Have you gone through anything yet?" Dylan asked.

Frankie shook her head, her lips thinning as she pressed them together. "I couldn't get myself past this point."

When Dylan's mother had passed away fourteen years ago, she had frozen up too when she went into her mother's empty house. The only way she got anything done was with the help of her kids and Evvie. And Frankie's situation was infinitely more complex than hers—Dylan couldn't fathom what emotions were running through Frankie's nervous system right now.

"If something is overwhelming," Dylan started, "I find it easiest to break it down into baby steps. Why don't we take the house one room at a time?"

"That seems practical." Frankie nodded. "Where should we start?"

"The top down, maybe? Or the bottom up? I'm not sure which would be easiest for you."

The house was quiet, so Dylan heard Frankie slow down her breathing. She didn't push her to decide, knowing that these things took time.

After a long thirty seconds or so, Frankie said, "I think I'd like to start upstairs. Ma's room is probably the least personal for me. I never went in there as a kid, and I barely knew her."

"Okay." It was strange to think that Dylan knew Ms. Wong better than Frankie did. "Do you want to go up together? Or should I grab a few boxes and meet you up there?"

"Can you meet me?" Frankie's eyebrows had drawn together slightly, just enough to crease the skin above her nose. At Dylan's nod, she turned and walked upstairs, her socked feet whispering against the hardwood floor.

Dylan looked around the living room. The furniture was familiar to her. Ms. Wong had a new TV, but the couch had been the same since she was a teenager, as were the chairs. The coffee table was the same too, a dent in one corner reminding Dylan of when she used to have tea here. She'd stare at that dent when she couldn't think of anything to say; she'd always had a problem of blurting her thoughts without thinking, and having something to focus on helped her keep her tongue in line.

There were a few photos on the walls and in frames on the side tables. Wing Keung's face shone out of most of them, along with Shirley's and their son's. None of those pictures were surprising. What *did* surprise her was a photo of Frankie framed and hung on the wall over the side table closest to the dining room. She hadn't seen it before, but then again, she hadn't been over for dinner in a few years, and she hadn't gone through the living room when she emptied the fridge. The photo was Frankie's headshot for work—the one that popped up if you searched her name online. Not that Dylan had searched her name much. In the photo, Frankie wore khaki shorts and a vest, her hair longer than it was now and pulled into a side ponytail. A camera strap was around her neck, and she held the camera at her side. Joy shone in her eyes.

Dylan's gaze landed on the family shrine set up just around the corner in the dining room. Multiple black-and-white photos stood on the small table, all framed and a bit dusty. A candle, drips of solid wax clinging its sides, had been placed in front of them. Her chest tightened a bit at the lack of flame on that candle; it had been important for the flame to stay lit. As a teenager, Frankie had gotten in trouble more than once for letting the flame go out.

A noise upstairs caught Dylan's attention. She had probably given Frankie enough time, anyway, so she pulled her eyes away from the photos and went up the stairs. As she got closer to the top, she heard something that sounded like a sniffle. Then a hiccup, maybe?

Something didn't seem quite right, so she increased her pace. Although she hadn't been upstairs since she was in her early twenties, she knew exactly which room was Ms. Wong's because it had been off limits every time she came over.

The door was half closed as if Frankie had pushed it slightly shut. When Dylan peered around the door, she didn't see Frankie at first. The light wasn't on, but sunlight streamed in through the window, making the space seem warm and inviting. Ms. Wong's bed was perfectly made, the white-and-green striped quilt smooth. There was a lamp on each night table, both with cream-colored shades, and a hairbrush sat on a vanity table to the foot of the bed on the opposite wall. The perfume smell was stronger in here.

Dylan stepped past the door and almost tripped over Frankie sitting on the carpeted floor. Her shoulders shook, and at first Dylan thought she was laughing. Then Frankie sucked in a shaky inhale, and Dylan realized she was very much *not* laughing.

"Hey," she said, crouching down and putting a hand on Frankie's back. Her knees cracked, and she winced, lowering herself to the floor as carefully as she could. She rubbed small circles on Frankie's back the way she used to when her girls were little and they couldn't fall asleep. "What's wrong?"

Frankie didn't answer, and as Dylan pushed the door shut more so she could see what Frankie was looking at, she got an idea of what had made Frankie so upset.

A low bookshelf sat against the wall in front of Frankie; her knees were practically pushed into it where she was sitting. The entire bookshelf was full of *National Geographic* magazines, the lineup of yellow spines a shock of color in the otherwise muted room.

Dear Library Board,

I used to think reading romance books was shameful. There are so many stereotypes about romance books: they're trashy, they're all about sex, they're beach reads, they don't talk about important things, etc. It took me a while to realize that most of that isn't true, and even if it is, it doesn't matter. Romance can be trashy, and it can have a lot of sex, and of course you can read it on the beach, but none of that's bad. Plus, plenty of romance books address important topics.

The library helped me embrace romance. I found a community of romance readers there, and I found so many books that I love on library shelves. Libraries help us find ourselves and realize that there are others like us out there. Libraries help us feel like we belong, and the Juniper Creek Library did that for me.

From,
Olivia Klassen
Owner of the Bluebell B&B

CHAPTER FIFTEEN

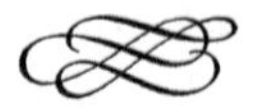

FRANKIE

Frankie didn't want Dylan to see her like this, but there was no helping it now. Thankfully, Dylan didn't say anything. She rubbed circles on Frankie's back and let her cry until she was spent. It could have been five minutes or an hour—Frankie had no idea how long she sat there, her tears falling onto the magazine in her hands.

One of her photographs stared up at her from the open page. It showed a lion basking on a rock in the sun, her cubs on the ground below her in the shade. They had been playing with each other as she snapped the photo, and one of them had its paw raised as if to swat the other, which it probably did as soon as the shutter clicked. The photo was a snapshot of family, of playfulness and ease.

Her face sticky with tears, Frankie sniffed. "I need a tissue," she said, shifting a bit. Her knees were stiff, and she was grateful when Dylan left so she could adjust her position. She pushed herself to her feet and sat on the edge of Ma's bed, still staring at the shelf full of *National Geographic* magazines.

"Here," Dylan said, coming back with a box of tissues.

Frankie blew her nose and cleaned herself up as best as she

could. The bed depressed as Dylan sat down beside her, leaving a bit of space between them.

Swallowing hard, Frankie said, "I didn't know she kept these." She blew out a breath through her mouth, trying not to burst into tears again. "I thought . . . I thought she wanted nothing to do with me." Another sniffle. "She never called, she never sent a letter . . . I thought she never wanted to see me again."

Dylan reached for her, rubbing her back once more. It was a bad idea, but Frankie leaned into the pressure. She liked that Dylan was touching her, even if it was only to comfort her. She had missed her touch more than she would admit to herself—all those times they had hugged or held hands as best friends do.

Dylan's voice was soft, the low tone of it soothing when she asked, "Did Wing Keung never say anything to you about your mom missing you?"

Frankie shook her head. "No. He might not even know about these." She held up the magazine in her hands then let it flop closed on her lap. "He did sort of tell me at lunch after the funeral, though . . ." Her throat thickened, and she struggled to get the words out. Maybe her brother did know after all. But then why hadn't he told her?

"What did he say at lunch?"

When Frankie turned to look at Dylan, her face was much closer than she had anticipated. Dylan's eyes were such a light blue that they were almost gray. Before Frankie had seen icebergs, that's the color she imagined they were, and she wasn't that far off depending on the light. That was one of her favorite things about Dylan—how her eyes could look dark and stormy or like a cloudy sky on a summer day.

Dylan tilted her head a bit closer when Frankie didn't answer, and she reached forward, twining her fingers with Frankie's. The sleeve of Dylan's blue plaid shirt was long enough to brush Frankie's skin. She had the urge to bury her nose in it, to see what Dylan smelled like now.

She flicked her eyes back to Dylan's, her gaze unnervingly intimate. "He said he wanted me to try and see Ma for who she truly was. I'm not sure what he meant, but . . . maybe this is part of it."

If Dylan got any closer, Frankie didn't know what would happen. Her heart was beating hard, and her thoughts weren't solely on Ma anymore. She could feel her attraction to Dylan like a string tying the two of them together, but she couldn't let that string form again. She was going back to France, and her ties here had already been cut.

She pulled her hand out of Dylan's, regretting it as soon as her hand was free. She must have imagined the flash of disappointment on Dylan's face.

"It could be," Dylan said, and it took Frankie a moment to remember what she was responding to. "Your mom didn't talk about you much, at least to me. But I know she still loved you." She gestured at the yellow magazines. "I'd say this is pretty damning evidence."

"Maybe." Frankie wiped her damp cheeks. "Let's start here, with the packing up. Do you think anyone will want these? Could the library use them? Or should I recycle them all?"

Dylan bit her lip. "Why don't we box them up, then you can decide what to do with them later."

Frankie nodded and looked around for a box.

"Oh, shoot," Dylan said. "I left the boxes downstairs. I'll go get them."

As Dylan went to get a few boxes, Frankie started pulling the magazines off the shelves. There were so many of them; she knew she had taken a lot of photos in her career, but seeing a physical collection of her work like this was surreal. Knowing that her mother had collected these was even more surreal. She made a mental note to call Wing Keung and confront him about this—she could have used some preparation before walking into it.

It took her and Dylan ten minutes to box up the magazines. Once the boxes were taped and labeled, they stacked them against the wall in Ma's room. Frankie's life's work in a tower of cardboard.

Dylan put her hands on her hips and looked at the boxes. "Hugo can help carry these downstairs. No reason for us to do it."

"Okay. You don't have to help me with the rest," Frankie said, nudging one of the boxes with her toe. "I'm glad you were here for moral support, but I can't see anything being more difficult than what just happened."

Dylan raised her eyebrows. "You want to clean out the rest of the house by yourself? I know you're here for another few weeks, but that's a lot of work. I don't mind helping. I have a truck, so I can take boxes for you. And I also know a lot of people around town besides Hugo who can help move the furniture."

Frankie's instinct was to say that she didn't need help. She was already feeling more attached to Dylan than she should; if she kept that up, she was bound to get heartbroken again. Every time she got too close to someone, it ended badly.

Leaving fifty years ago had been only the beginning.

Dylan sat on the bed, and a waft of air tickled Frankie's nose, bringing with it the smell of Ma's perfume. Her chest constricted. She didn't want to clean this house. She wanted to get out and take photos, to immerse herself in nature again and get away from all the emotions floating around this town. If she let people help her, the cleaning would go faster.

"Alright," she said. "You've convinced me. I think I want to start somewhere easier, though. Maybe the kitchen?"

Dylan shrugged, and without a word the two of them went to the kitchen. Someone had been by earlier to clean out the fridge, which Frankie was grateful for. She could handle decomposing animals, mold, and fungi, but she did not want to encounter any of it in her mother's refrigerator.

"I'll run out and get tissue paper and bubble wrap," Dylan said.

While she was gone, Frankie unpacked the cupboards. Most of the dishes were familiar to her, but she didn't feel any connection to them. Instead she was inquisitive, turning each dish over in her hands and wondering what memories were archived within it. She got herself into a rhythm of pulling out and stacking dishes, and the sound of the front door opening made her jump.

"I brought lunch," Dylan called from the entryway. "I hope you still like sandwiches." She came into the kitchen with a few bags slung over her arms. "I got premade ones from Juniper Foods, plus two bottles of water. The tap water hasn't improved since you left."

Touched at the gesture, Frankie smiled. "Thank you." Her chest felt lighter now that her discovery from earlier had settled in her mind. Her bitterness toward her mother hadn't evaporated, but there was curiosity there too, like she was willing to see if maybe she was wrong about Ma. Part of her hoped she was, even if that would make everything hurt more.

Dylan passed her a boxed sandwich and a bottle of water then pulled out one of the chairs at the kitchen table and opened her own.

Frankie sat down as well. "Why wouldn't I like sandwiches anymore?" she asked.

"I don't know. Maybe your world travels made you more cultured, and you no longer eat meat and bread." She took a large bite of her own meat and bread.

Frankie snorted. "I think you overestimate how fancy photographers are. Many of my photoshoots were out in the middle of the wilderness where there wasn't exactly a stove or even a microwave, much less a refrigerator. I think I survived off protein bars for years."

"Well then, you're welcome for the gourmet food."

Frankie laughed and bit into her sandwich. "Thank you again for doing this," she said after a sip of water.

Dylan waved a hand. "Don't mention it," she said around a mouthful of sandwich. She swallowed then added, "Seriously, don't. Otherwise, I might reconsider and let you do it all yourself."

The two of them grinned at each other. This banter felt easy, familiar. It washed away some of the awkwardness that had been between them earlier that day.

They spent the rest of the afternoon wrapping dishes in bubble wrap and boxing them up so they could be donated, then they moved on to the pantry and went through all the food there. They talked as they worked, learning more about each other, and a warmth grew in Frankie's chest whenever she looked at Dylan.

Dylan offered to pick up the dishes and the food the next evening and take them to a shelter or charity shop, and Frankie took her up on the offer since she didn't have a car to do it herself.

On their way out just before dinner, Frankie took one last look at the growing stack of boxes in the living room. She may have been packing up her mother's life, but she had a feeling that she was just starting to unpack her own.

CHAPTER SIXTEEN

DYLAN

After helping Frankie pack a few things on Monday, it seemed natural for Dylan to handle the boxes for her. Neither of them wanted to risk their backs, so she enlisted Hugo as their heavy lifter when he wasn't working. Dylan offered to help with more packing too, but Frankie said she, Margie, and Gem had it covered.

The pang of disappointment in Dylan's chest was not welcome, and she tried to push it down. So what if other people were helping Frankie? It's not like Dylan had a monopoly on her time or even *wanted* to spend much time with her.

She just wanted to figure out where they stood with each other after what had happened on Monday. She was sure there had been something between them. When Frankie found those magazines, Dylan had seen her pain. She had been so vulnerable, shaking with sobs under Dylan's hands. Experiences like that were supposed to bring people together, weren't they?

And yet Frankie seemed content to smile and wave at her, and not much else, as Hugo helped load boxes into Dylan's truck.

There was no conversation, no discussion about what had happened.

That was Frankie's prerogative, and yet Dylan ached for more.

Not that she would ever admit that out loud. The raffle was on Saturday, and that was where her focus needed to be.

~

ON FRIDAY MORNING after Dylan took the dogs for a walk, she ended up in the library. Hugo scowled at her when she walked in. "What are you doing here on your day off?" he asked, his hands on his hips.

The truth was that Frankie hadn't asked Dylan to help with the house today, and she hadn't made other plans just in case, so she wasn't sure what to do with herself. What she told Hugo was "I want to make sure everything is set up and ready to go for tomorrow."

He sucked his teeth. "You don't know how to take a break, do you? I've worked with you for three years now, and I don't think you've gone on vacation or taken a day off just to do something for you. What are your hobbies?"

Dylan raised her eyebrows. "You work for me, you know, not the other way around."

"Technically, I work for the board, not for you. And I *care* about you, Dylan. I'm being nice."

"Are you?" She narrowed her eyes at him. "I have plenty of hobbies, and they're none of your business. I'm going to my office."

He rolled his eyes at her and mumbled something under his breath that sounded like "Useless."

In her office on the computer, Dylan opened the shared document Hugo had created to keep track of all their fundraising activities. The volunteers had access to the document as well and could check off what was done and what wasn't. Jamie was getting them a portable debit machine for the raffle, and Vera, Eleanor, and Minnie were going to run the table, with Iris on standby in case one of them needed a break.

Charlie, Kat's best friend, had made a note that she'd

contacted a news station in Abbotsford, and they were sending a reporter and a camera for the festival kick-off. A smile spread over Dylan's face—like Minnie had said, media coverage would be a big help.

Dylan's smile faded as she read over the rest of the document. There was nothing there for her to do. She didn't even need to show up the next day if she didn't want to, but she would, of course.

She sighed. Evvie, Eleanor, and Minnie were at work, so there was no one for her to visit. Usually, on a day like today, she'd curl up in her backyard with a good book. She had one on the go about a reporter and a celebrity falling head over heels for each other, which was a fun read. It was still warm enough to read outside, and Darcy and Bingley would love to spend the day running around and rolling in the grass. But she was too restless for that. How could she sit still with everything going on?

Without questioning her own motivations too much, she strode out of the library and over to the Bluebell. She hadn't been inside the place since she dropped off a stack of romance novels for Olivia a few months ago, but it looked the same. Olivia stood at the welcome desk, flipping through a large leather ledger. Her blouse was striped today—green and orange—and it clashed loudly with the wallpaper. "Oh, Dylan," she said, looking up. "What a nice surprise! What can I do for you?"

"Is Frankie in?" Dylan asked.

"I think she left to work on the house already," Olivia said. "She told me you've been helping her. You two know each other, right? From when she used to live here?"

"Yeah," Dylan said. The phrase "know each other" seemed like a grand understatement. "Thanks."

She turned and marched out the door with Olivia calling, "Oh, okay, bye!" behind her.

As she walked to Ms. Wong's house, she forced herself to slow down. What the fuck was she doing? Frankie hadn't asked her for help, and if she showed up, she'd likely be barging in where she wasn't wanted. But a door had opened on Monday, and she needed it to either close altogether or swing wide open.

Against her better judgement, she wanted to nudge it open more.

The lights were on in the house when she got there, and she heard footsteps when she rapped on the door. A few seconds later, Frankie opened it. She was wearing joggers and a nondescript blue T-shirt; it was the most comfortable outfit Dylan had seen her in since she'd been back in town. She had dust in her hair and beads of sweat on her forehead.

"Dylan," she said, swiping a hand over her eyebrows. "Hi."

"I thought maybe you could use some help," Dylan said.

"Um." Frankie glanced over her shoulder then back to Dylan. "I suppose I could. Come in." She stepped back and allowed Dylan to move past her.

Frankie had opened the living room windows and presumably the ones in the kitchen as well; a cool breeze flowed throughout the house, and the smells of grass and crisp fall air overtook the lingering perfume and incense. All the photos and decor had been taken off the walls, and the living room was rather bare. The furniture was still there, but the place no longer looked lived in.

"I was going through the spare room," Frankie said. "I don't think Ma went in there much. There was a lot of dust, and the closet was full of closed boxes of photo albums and old documents." She gestured to a stack of boxes by the wall. "Wing Keung is coming to pick them up on Sunday. Dean, from the Bluebell, took all the other heavy boxes that Hugo didn't grab."

Dylan nodded. "That's good. It looks like you're making quick work of the rest of the house."

"All that's left is my old room and the bigger pieces of furniture."

"You haven't cleaned out your room yet?"

Frankie shook her head, and Dylan reached out to pull a cobweb from above her ear. As she leaned over, the space between them crackled with energy. She took an extra step back as she shook the cobweb from her fingers. "Thanks," Frankie said quietly. She straightened her T-shirt then continued, "After what happened in Ma's room, I've been wary of going into my own. It feels strange to even call it *mine* still. But . . . since you're here, would you like to go in with me?"

Dylan ran a hand through her hair. "Sure." Frankie may not have wanted her help with packing up the rest of the small stuff, but it meant something that Dylan got to help with the most intimate rooms. At least, that's what she told herself. If Frankie didn't want her here, she wouldn't have let her in in the first place.

"Okay, just a minute. I need a drink."

While Frankie got a glass of water, Dylan looked around the living room again like she had on Monday. The house seemed so impersonal now, and it was sad in a way. How easy it was to erase someone's presence. If there were no photos, no belongings, no physical traces of someone, all that was left were memories. And memories were fickle.

"Would you mind going up first this time?" Frankie asked as she came back to join Dylan. "I don't want a repeat of last time."

"Sure." Dylan went up the stairs and had the odd feeling that she was a teenager again, going upstairs to study with Frankie.

The door to Frankie's old room was closed, and the knob made a crunching noise when Dylan turned it, as if that door wasn't opened often. Dylan gasped as the room came into view.

"What is it?" Frankie asked in the hallway behind her.

Dylan reached to flick the light on, and it took her a second to find the switch. "Christ, Frankie . . . it's like you never left."

"What?" Frankie put her hand on Dylan's arm and leaned past her to see. "Oh my god."

It was like stepping back in time. The twin bed Frankie had slept in sat against the wall under the window where it had always sat, her white quilt with pink flowers still draped over the mattress. The pink decorative cushion Frankie used to lean on when she read was still there too, slightly faded and propped against the pillows.

Two wooden night tables framed the bed in a reflection of Ms. Wong's room, with a lamp on only one of them instead of on both. Frankie's white dresser was still against the other wall, and the walls . . . they were plastered with photographs. Some were portraits, but most were black-and-white or faded pictures that Frankie had cut out of newspapers and magazines. Dylan used to search through magazines for photographs for her, even going so far as to rip pages out of them at the store without buying them.

Frankie moved into the room without a word and ran her fingers over the photos above the dresser. "I remember cutting these out," she said. Her finger moved over one of a woman standing on a table, and she laughed. "Do you remember this one?" she asked Dylan over her shoulder. "We found this one together. We said we'd be like her one day—standing up for our rights."

Dylan stepped up beside her. "I remember," she said, grinning. "We thought it was risky just to put it on your wall."

"But it's still here." There was a smile in Frankie's voice. "I wonder why Ma left everything. She could have turned this into a sewing room or an office or whatever she wanted."

"She loved you," Dylan said softly, looking at Frankie's profile. The curve of her ear, the shadow of her cheekbone, the laugh lines by the corner of her eye. Something in her was melting at the joy and nostalgia on Frankie's face. "You might have left, but I don't think she forgot you. How could she? Those magazines, and this"—she waved her hand around the room—"preservation of time. I think she knew you were a magnificent person, Frankie. I think, in some way, she was waiting for you to come back."

Frankie turned to her, an intensity in her eyes that hadn't been there before. Before she knew what she was doing, Dylan stepped forward until there was only a breath of space between them.

CHAPTER SEVENTEEN

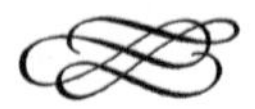

FRANKIE

Frankie's attention was torn between finding her room unchanged and how close Dylan was standing to her.

As Frankie had cleaned out the house over the week, she had discovered multiple clues that Ma hadn't hated her like she'd thought. And Margie had told her about how often Ma had talked about Frankie—she read any article Frankie was mentioned in, and she was always showing Margie Frankie's photos. "I didn't think you'd want to know," Margie had said. "I'm sorry. I should have told you."

Frankie had had time to come to terms with it, to regret staying away but also to grow in anger toward her mother. Why hadn't she called? Why hadn't she ever reached out? Frankie couldn't be upset with Margie because it wasn't Margie's place to say anything, but Wing Keung could have said something. When he came to pick up the boxes on Sunday, she was going to bring it up. But that was a problem for later.

Dylan was right in front of her now, her gray-blue eyes a storm. Frankie was surprised no lightning flickered in her irises when she could practically feel bolts of it flashing between them. Her breath was like thunder in her ears as Dylan took a step closer.

She had called her *magnificent.* She'd said Ma had been waiting for her to come back.

"Were you waiting, too?" Frankie said, her voice so low it was almost a whisper. Her pulse pounded in her ears. "Were you waiting for me to come back?"

Dylan didn't answer with words. She lifted a hand and ran the backs of her fingers lightly down the side of Frankie's face, trailing down her neck like a breath of wind.

Frankie shivered under Dylan's touch, but it wasn't unpleasant. No one had touched her like this—with such tenderness—in years. She hadn't let them. Every time she let someone in, let them close enough to touch her, she was disappointed. They weren't Dylan.

When they were teenagers, she and Dylan had spent hours together in this room, studying or listening to music or putting photos on the walls. So many times, Frankie had held herself back, wanting to be as close to Dylan as she was now.

That hadn't been possible then. But things had changed.

Words were needed now, so many words. Why hadn't Dylan contacted her if she'd wanted her to come back? The question caught in Frankie's throat, and she leaned forward, crushing her mouth against Dylan's.

Time froze for a second then sped up until it was charging ahead like a freight train.

Dylan's hands were in her hair, her foot pushing between both of Frankie's, and all thoughts flew out of Frankie's mind. She let herself get lost in the feeling of Dylan's chest pressed against hers, and she slid her hands up the back of Dylan's shirt as Dylan pushed her backward toward the bed.

Only when she was lying flat with Dylan's weight on top of her did her eyes fly open and her brain kick back into gear. "Wait," she panted, pushing on Dylan's chest. "What are we doing?"

Dylan's face was flushed, her silvery-purple hair sticking up like she'd just rolled out of bed. Her lips were slightly swollen, her eyes still stormy. She pushed herself up and moved back against the dresser, her chest heaving. "Sorry," she said. "I don't know."

Looking around the room, Frankie began to laugh. "We're in our seventies," she said. "We come in here like we've stepped back in time, and now we're acting like it, like we've been turned into teenagers."

Dylan was laughing now too, but Frankie's laughter turned into something else. The tears running down her face were no longer mirthful, but mournful. Maybe Ma had been leaving the door open for Frankie, but Frankie had never seen it.

"Oh shit." Dylan must have realized that Frankie was no longer laughing. She rushed over to the side of the bed. "Come here," she said, scooching to the middle and leaning against the headboard. She opened her arms, and Frankie crawled into them, resting her head on Dylan's chest as she cried.

This was the second time in one week that Dylan had seen her break down. And the second time in one week that Dylan had opened up to her, had comforted her in a way that made her feel wanted. "Why does this keep happening?" Frankie said, sniffling. "I'm getting snot on your shirt."

Dylan huffed out a laugh. "This keeps happening because it's not easy to lose a parent. And I don't give a fuck about my shirt."

There were so many emotions threatening to burst out of Frankie's chest that she ignored her brain's protests at what she was doing. Dylan was warm, and here, and safe, and Frankie needed her.

She didn't know how long she cried for, but at some point Dylan had started rubbing her back again. Frankie closed her eyes and Dylan shifted down so they were both lying flat, one of Dylan's arms holding Frankie close. Dylan smelled clean and faintly like lilacs, and Frankie relaxed into the smell. Her head started to pound from crying, so she deepened her breath and felt Dylan match her rhythm. Dylan's heartbeat was one of the most comforting sounds she'd ever heard.

~

FRANKIE BATTED her eyelids open and squinted at the photo-covered wall in front of her. Where was she? It looked like her bedroom . . . Her pillow shifted under her and she sat up, a bolt of pain going through her head. She wiped a line of drool off her cheek.

Dylan stirred again and yawned. "You drooled on me," she said, opening her eyes to look at Frankie. Was she *smirking*?

The realization that she'd been sleeping *on* Dylan made her want to bolt like a rabbit. "I was comfortable," Frankie said. "Although my arm went numb. Sorry about the drool."

Dylan sat up and groaned. "What time is it? I didn't mean to fall asleep."

"I'm not sure." Despite the nap, Frankie's head still pounded. And now there was a stale taste in her mouth and growing panic in her chest. "I need water."

She left the room before Dylan could say anything, wanting time to think and recover from . . . whatever had just happened.

In the kitchen, she picked up her glass of water from earlier. She didn't have any painkillers with her, so water would have to suffice for now.

The floor above her head creaked as Dylan presumably got up. Frankie kept her eyes trained out the window over the sink as she drank her water, searching for answers in the backyard. She and Dylan had just kissed for the first time, and her feelings were like whirlpools, swirling so fast that Frankie couldn't grasp them.

She heard Dylan come down the stairs. "Are you okay?" Dylan asked quietly from behind her.

Frankie continued staring straight ahead. She thought about lying, about saying *yes*, but she told the truth. "I don't know." It felt amazing to have Dylan touch her and hold her like she'd always imagined. They didn't know each other as well as they used to, but that was an opportunity more than anything.

But now that she had what she'd been longing for, it scared

her. She'd loved Dylan more than anyone else in her life, and that had burned her. Her wildest dreams were coming true, and that meant something horrible must be coming. If she got too close to Dylan now, maybe that horrible thing would be leaving her. Again.

But she had never planned on staying.

Dylan hadn't responded, so Frankie said, "I always wanted something like that to happen, but . . . I wasn't expecting it now. I don't know what it means, or what I want it to mean."

Dylan cleared her throat and said, "Okay." After a beat of silence, she added, "I'm going to go. If you need me or want to talk . . . you know where to find me."

A robin flew into the tree in the backyard, and Frankie kept her eyes on it. On its bright red belly, the way it flicked its tail feathers, the way it hopped on the bark.

Although she heard Dylan go to the front room, she couldn't bring herself to move. Her feet were rooted to the floor, and her fingers drifted to her lips as she remembered how Dylan's lips had felt on hers. How her skin had felt under Frankie's fingertips.

A few minutes later, the front door creaked open and shut, and Frankie was alone again.

CHAPTER EIGHTEEN

DYLAN

Sleep didn't come easily to Dylan these days, but Friday night was worse than most. The few times she dozed, she had fever dreams about waking up in Ms. Wong's house alone, searching for Frankie but not being able to find her. She got up at three to use the washroom and get a glass of water, and when she finally fell asleep again, she had a different dream involving Frankie that made her wake up longing for a cold shower.

Five-thirty was an early morning for her, but she couldn't lie in bed anymore thinking about how Frankie had kissed her yesterday. How they had almost done more than kiss. How Frankie had relaxed into her and fallen asleep.

It had meant something to Dylan, even if she didn't want it to. Even if Frankie didn't know what she wanted it to mean. Frankie had been the one who left all those years ago, the one who broke off their friendship. And yet if Frankie wanted Dylan now, Dylan didn't think she would say no.

It had been five decades—almost three-quarters of Dylan's life—since she and Frankie had known each other like Dylan knew *Pride and Prejudice*, and yet nothing had matched how Dylan had felt around Frankie. Not even her love with her ex-husband had been like that, but she hadn't known that anything else was possible. She hadn't known that she could have the same type of relationship with Frankie—a *better* one, even—and by the time she figured it out, it was too late.

She thought she'd never feel that thrill again, but Frankie was back, at least for a few weeks. Would Dylan let that time slip through her fingers? Maybe being with Frankie again would be self-sabotage, but like Hugo said, when did she ever take time for herself?

Her thoughts swirled in circles, part of her wanting to lean into spending time with Frankie and another part of her wanting to stay as far away from Frankie as possible. Especially since Frankie was leaving, and this time Dylan knew it.

Darcy and Bingley were more than happy to go for an early walk around the pond. It was cooler out, a soft mist rising over the water. Mornings like these reminded Dylan of moody Victorian novels where women lived in or visited Gothic mansions that were inevitably haunted, and someone always died. Or a wife was kept in an attic. Morbid, maybe, but pleasantly atmospheric.

Darcy squatted to do her business, so Dylan paused and waited. An odd clicking sound came from somewhere farther down the path. That was a strange sound for a bird to make. She stuck her hand in a bag to clean up Darcy's mess, and it hit her: That wasn't a bird. It was a camera.

How many people in Juniper Creek would be up this early taking photos? There was only one person Dylan could think of, and she wasn't sure she was ready to see her again right now. Not with that dream still fresh in her mind.

She considered turning back the way she came, then she steeled herself and let the dogs drag her forward. Evvie had scolded her for training them to lead, and now she saw why that was a problem; they weren't giving her near enough time to prepare for seeing Frankie again so soon.

Darcy and Bingley got to Frankie first, going right up to her to sniff at her pants, their tails wagging.

"Well, good morning," Frankie said, laughing, holding her

hands out to them while her camera hung around her neck. She bent over to give Bingley's ears a good scratch, then looked up and froze when she locked eyes with Dylan. "Dylan."

Dylan held up a hand. "That's my name." She shifted from foot to foot, not sure what to say to Frankie after what had happened between them the day before.

Frankie blinked, visibly flustered. "These are your dogs?" she asked, keeping her eyes on Bingley as she spoke. She was still scratching one of Bingley's ears and had reached over to scratch one of Darcy's as well.

"Yeah. Darcy and Bingley."

"*Pride and Prejudice*. Of course." Her words wavered slightly. She straightened up and Dylan did her best to pull the dogs back a bit. Which meant that they barely moved. "They're sweet."

Dylan cleared her throat. "They are. Take any good photos this morning?"

"I think so." Frankie held up her camera, looking at something on the display screen and very clearly *not* looking at Dylan. "Wildlife tends to be most active at dusk and dawn. The mist is pretty this morning, too."

"Mm-hmm." A question crawled up Dylan's throat about what had happened yesterday, but she kept her lips sealed. She'd given Frankie the opportunity to come to her when—and if—she was ready, and she wasn't going to force the subject.

Thankfully, the dogs were pulling at their harnesses again, ready to continue their walk. "That's my cue," she said, gesturing at the dogs. "You coming to Pumpkin Days this afternoon?"

Frankie looked up at her finally, a few strands of hair hanging in her eye. "I think so. I'm taking the day off from working at the house."

Her words were ripe with meaning, but Dylan didn't want to dig too much into it. "Probably a good idea. See you later then."

"See you."

Dylan was grateful for Darcy and Bingley's tendency to lead on their way home; she didn't think she'd have got there otherwise. Running into Frankie had her mentally reliving everything that had happened yesterday, and she kept thinking through Frankie's words: *I'm taking the day off from working on the house.* Was it because of what happened in Frankie's childhood bedroom? Was Dylan part of the past that Frankie was trying to clear out?

Frankie had seemed out of sorts, but Dylan didn't know how to read that.

If she didn't keep busy, her thoughts would overwhelm her. So she fed the dogs, showered, stuffed a muffin in her mouth, and headed to the library. She'd restock books and organize the holds shelf until they opened. That would occupy her enough to stay out of her own head.

~

DYLAN MET Evvie at the diner for lunch. "I can only stay for the kick-off, then I have to get back to the clinic," Evvie said. "We really need to get another receptionist. I can't keep answering the phone, helping clients, and running back to clean the rooms all at the same time. Did I tell you that Elouise Mitchell yelled at me the other day because I didn't ask her to pay fast enough? I couldn't! I was still waiting for the vet to put the items through." She sipped her water, her brows drawn together.

"That's rough, Ev, I'm sorry." Dylan took a bite of her pancakes. "I'm glad you get to see the kick-off, though."

"I should be able to see more of it. I'm the chair of the Friends, for the sake of all that glitters." She threw her hands up.

"I know. Have they interviewed anyone lately?"

"I don't know. They don't tell me these things. If they weren't so short-staffed, I would put in my notice." She speared a sausage as if it had personally harmed her.

Dylan raised her eyebrows. "Damn, Ev. You'd really quit? I thought you didn't want to retire."

"Yes, well"—Evvie bit into her sausage viciously—"I'm

getting tired of all this." She chewed, swallowed, and sighed. "Do you think Jamie would get me a jar of her secret sauce to cheer me up?" she asked.

Dylan shrugged. "Worth a try."

When they hailed Jamie over, she said, "I can't go around giving it out, Evvie. Everyone would be asking for it. But I'll bring you some to dip your sausage in. How's that?"

"Fine." After Jamie left, Evvie turned to Dylan again. "So what'd you do yesterday?"

Dylan shoved more pancake in her mouth to avoid answering right away. If she lied, Evvie would see right through her. So, she told the truth, glossing over the gritty details. Her heartbeat picked up speed as she spoke, and she fumbled over her words. Romance hadn't been in her books for years, and it was painfully unfamiliar territory.

Evvie brightened up as soon as she recounted Frankie kissing her. "This is better than secret sauce," she said, leaning forward with her elbows on the table. "Did you kiss her back?"

Dylan told her the rest, her throat tightening as she mentioned how Frankie had practically fled from the bedroom. "She said she didn't know if she wanted it to mean something, though," she finished. "I have to be okay if it didn't. Mean something, I mean."

Sitting back in her seat, Evvie nodded. "So it meant something to you?"

Dylan looked at her best friend from under her eyebrows. "What do you think?" How could it *not* mean something to her?

A grin took over Evvie's face. "I know. I can hear it in your voice." Her eyes went shiny. "I really hope it works out for you two. This is your second chance to be together. You're not married, your kids are grown up, you're both independent. And now you know you're gay. It's perfect."

"You're such a fucking sap," Dylan said, although she loved that about Evvie, and her best friend knew it. She wasn't wrong about the situation either—this was a chance for them to be together. But Frankie wasn't here for long, so if something did happen between them, it likely wouldn't be permanent. Could Dylan handle that? Could Frankie?

Evvie looked at her watch, the rainbow band sparkling in the diner's lights. "We should go. Lorelai will start her kick-off speech soon."

They paid their bill then walked over to the park. The kick-off for most town events happened at the gazebo, and Lorelai stood there already, waiting for the right time. Around her, the park was teeming with people waiting to begin the festivities, mostly parents with their kids. There were multiple stations set up for different games like the three-legged race and the mummy wrap. Dylan spotted Kat and Charlie at a face-painting booth, and Minnie and Eleanor sat at a table beneath an orange pop-up tent. Vera straightened the banner on the table front that read "Library Raffle." Kat and Charlie had made it with their school friends, the words painted in black and orange with watercolor leaves around them.

A reporter in a smart gray suit stood off to the side with a cameraperson, their camera trained on the gazebo. They were going to interview Iris later about the Pumpkin Days events and the fundraising efforts for the library. Iris had asked Dylan to join her for the interview, but Dylan had declined. She was not one for the limelight.

Evvie and Dylan said hello to their friends at the booth and stood beside it as Lorelai began her speech.

"Hello, everyone!" she said into a microphone. Her voice crackled through a few portable speakers set up around the park. "Welcome to the kick-off for Juniper Creek's annual Pumpkin Days festival!"

The adults clapped and many of the children screamed or jumped around with an abundance of energy. Watching them, Dylan was reminded of why she usually avoided the games day of the festival; the only children she wanted to be around these days were her grandchildren, which was why Gwen oversaw story time.

Lorelai continued, "I would like to acknowledge and reflect on the land we are standing on as we enjoy the games today. Juniper Creek is part of the traditional and unceded territories of the Stó:lō people, the Semá:th and Máthxwi First Nation. These people—my ancestors—are the original caretakers of this land, and we respect the relationship that Indigenous Nations have with this land. As we live, play, and work here, we are committed to respecting and learning from Indigenous communities."

After another round of applause, she said, "Thank you all for joining me here on this gorgeous fall day. Please feel free to play as many games as you want. We also have face-painting and snacks available, and I encourage you to stop by the raffle table to raise funds for our local library. Happy Pumpkin Days!"

The crowd cheered then dispersed, parents trying their best to keep track of their little ones. Dylan scanned the park but couldn't see Frankie anywhere. A few people meandered toward the raffle booth, so Evvie and Dylan moved back to give them more space.

"Are you going to stay here?" Evvie asked, looking at her watch again. "I need to get back to work."

"I should probably get back to the library. Hovering here isn't going to make the numbers rise," Dylan said with a sigh. "I'll go back in a minute."

"Okey dokey. See you tomorrow for dinner?"

"Wouldn't miss it."

Evvie kissed her cheek then speed walked back toward the library parking lot where she had parked her yellow Bug. Dylan waited until people had cleared out from the table, and she reapproached to ask if she could help in any way.

"We've got it covered," Vera said, waving her off. "The debit machine is working, the spreadsheet you set up is working. Everything is fine."

"And we can count," Eleanor said, her eyes twinkling.

"Okay, smartass," Dylan said, scowling at her friend good-naturedly.

Minnie, who was shoving tickets into the raffle box, blinked up at her. "Even though I know you better now, it never fails to surprise me that a librarian swears." Her frown suggested that she didn't approve.

Dylan shrugged. "I don't swear at work." At least, she tried not to.

After her friends reassured her once again that they were set for success, Dylan went back to the library. Gwen was on shift today, but the library was almost empty. Everyone was likely over at the park or taking advantage of the nice weather to shop on Main Street.

Dylan went to grab the blue book cart, the one with the broken wheel, when she spotted a familiar face in the nonfiction section that made her heart skip. "Can I help you?" she asked.

Frankie looked up, her eyebrows raising when she saw Dylan. "I'm looking for a book on local birds," she said. "Do you happen to have any?"

"I can find you one."

Frankie followed her over to the front desk.

"You missed the festival kick-off," Dylan said, trying not to sound accusatory, as she opened the browser.

"No, I didn't." There was laughter in Frankie's eyes when Dylan glanced up at her. "I left just before you did. I saw you at the raffle booth. Everything looked like it was running smoothly."

Dylan kept her gaze on the screen as she said, "I hope so." Knowing that Frankie had been at the kick-off made her oddly pleased. "Okay, we've got a couple of books you might be interested in." She jotted down the call numbers on a notepad and took it with her back to the nonfiction section. It took only a minute for her to find the right books. "Want me to check them out under my account for you?"

Frankie smiled at her, just about melting her heart. "I'd appreciate that."

"Okay. Back to the desk we go."

As she scanned the first book, Frankie said, "I was thinking of booking a table at the market on the last weekend of Pumpkin Days. Do you think people would be interested in buying professional photos of local wildlife?"

"Definitely. People around here would love to buy your work." Including herself. Frankie's cheeks turned the softest shade of pink, and Dylan wanted to feel her skin again. Instead, she slid over the two books about birds. "Here."

"Thank you." Frankie put the books in her satchel. "On that subject, I have a favor to ask."

"Okay, shoot." Dylan knew she'd say yes, whatever the favor was, even if it was a bad idea. Even if Frankie hadn't said a word about their kiss yet.

"I was hoping to photograph wildlife outside of town, but as you know, I don't have a car. Would you be willing to drive me out of town one day this week so I can take some shots?"

When they were younger, Dylan had loved watching Frankie take photos. She was in her element, and her passion was evident in her every move. And now she was asking Dylan to go with her, to see that again now that Frankie had years of professional experience. Dylan had to restrain her enthusiasm when she said, "I can do that. I've got Monday off again, if that works."

She had planned to write up an advertisement for the scavenger hunt on Monday since the deadline for it was on Tuesday, but she'd have plenty of time to do that either before her weekly dinner on Sunday, or after driving Frankie out to take pictures.

"It does. Thank you. You've been so helpful." Frankie shouldered her satchel, clearly getting ready to leave.

"No problem. See you Monday?"

Dylan watched Frankie walk out the sliding doors, then she sagged against the desk. She prayed to all the gods and goddesses she could think of that Frankie asking her for help meant that their kiss had meant something to her.

If it didn't, Dylan was in for a world of pain. She was falling for Frankie again, and there was no denying it.

Dear Library Board,

I know you don't really have control over whether the library stays open, but these letters will hopefully show you how much the library means to the citizens of Juniper Creek.

To me, the library is a place of learning and opportunity. It helps people find jobs, it offers courses and resources, and it's a safe space for the community to gather. It's more accessible than most other public services, and it has free programs for people of all ages. Everyone is welcome there, and that's what has always drawn me to libraries.

Every librarian I know is committed to growing and changing and making the world a better place. If our library stays open, that's what will happen: the world will become better.

Thank you for taking the time to read this letter and the letters from other library patrons. We appreciate your time and what you do for libraries across the region.

From,
Evvie Adler
Chair, Friends of the Juniper Creek Library

CHAPTER NINETEEN

FRANKIE

Frankie woke up at dawn on Sunday to thoughts of Dylan. Dylan's lips on hers. Her hands under Dylan's shirt, the two of them pawing at each other like horny teenagers. What happened the other day—in her childhood bedroom, no less—had thrown her off. She hadn't known how to react to it in the moment, and Dylan hadn't pushed her when she said she didn't know if it meant something.

But it did. Frankie wanted to resist it; she was only here for a few weeks, after all. Usually, she wouldn't say no to a fling, but Dylan was different. Dylan was not a three-week whirlwind romance.

At the same time, though, she couldn't deny that the restlessness she'd felt since leaving Juniper Creek fifty years ago had abated since she'd been back here.

When Frankie chose to be a wildlife photographer, she could have stayed in Canada. No one told her she had to travel, and National Geographic would have been happy to have her specialize in one area. Every time she tried to settle down, though, on her own or with someone else, she got itchy. At first, she thought it was pure wanderlust, but something else had been driving her. After traveling for decades, she figured that maybe settling down in a quiet place like France would finally scratch the itch. And yet she'd still felt it there, to the point that her clothes were still packed in her suitcase.

It was only once she had come here again, to Juniper Creek, that the itch started to go away. Sure, she'd been uncomfortable at Ma's funeral, but since then she'd started to settle in. Now that she'd been here just over two weeks, she should have been aching to get on a plane again, but she wasn't. And she couldn't deny that Dylan was a vital part of that.

That's partially why she'd asked Dylan to drive her out of town. She needed to express her feelings somehow, and time together in nature could help her do that.

Rolling out of bed, she decided to go for a walk like she had the day before. Strolling in the fresh air would ground her.

There was no mist this morning, but it was drizzling, which made for beautiful photos of glistening raindrops, their surfaces stretched and perfectly round where they rested on leaves and fence posts. She didn't run into Dylan or her dogs, and the disappointment that washed through her was not entirely unexpected. She wanted space to think, and yet she wanted to see Dylan too.

By the time she got back to the Bluebell, she still had an hour or so until her breakfast date with her brother at the diner; he was coming to pick up the boxes from Ma's. To fill her time, Frankie brought one of the bird books into the Bluebell's lobby.

"Good morning," Dean said, coming over to her. His long blond hair was in a high bun, making him look similar to a Viking. All that was missing was the beard and the outfit. "Would you like a coffee? Food?"

"No food, thanks. I'm meeting my brother for breakfast. A coffee would be great, though."

"Gotcha." He winked at her then headed back to the kitchen.

Frankie flipped through the bird book, looking for birds she could find in the area at this time of year. It was enjoyable to photograph mammals, but birds were by far the most fun. She'd always loved the elegance with which they moved. They could be so graceful but also ridiculous, especially during their mating rituals, and birds displayed all the colors of the rainbow.

The red-crowned crane was Frankie's favorite. She may not have had many connections to her Chinese roots, but every time she saw a red-crowned crane, she felt a spark of admiration. Phoenixes were more popular in Chinese mythology, but something about the crane's clean lines and the splash of red on their heads appealed to Frankie. She could watch them all day, and she did once when she went to Japan.

Dean dropped off her coffee, and she thanked him with a wave. Putting the book on her lap, she picked up the steaming mug and looked out the front window. As her thoughts drifted to Dylan again, her cell phone rang, her ringtone of bird calls seeming to echo in the small lobby space. "Hello?" Frankie answered.

"I'm at the diner. Where are you?" Wing Keung said.

Frankie looked at her watch. Her thoughts must have drifted more than she'd meant them to. "I'll be right over," she said, already moving toward the kitchen with her half-empty mug.

Wing Keung was sitting at a booth, reading a newspaper, when Frankie joined him. One of the high schoolers who worked at the diner brought her coffee and took their orders.

"So, how's the cleaning going?" her brother asked.

"Good. All the smaller items are packed up. Now we need to get the furniture moved out. Did you want any of it?"

He shook his head. "Shirley and I went through the house before the funeral. We took a couple of decorative plates, but we don't need anything else."

A ping of annoyance sounded in Frankie's head that her brother had gone through the house but hadn't bothered to start packing anything for her. She took a deep breath, choosing her battles.

"Okay. Well, I have about five boxes for you now, so have fun looking through them." All the photos from the family shrine were in there along with a bunch of albums. Looking at the photos had made Frankie feel lonely; she knew the names of the people in the pictures and she knew she was related to them, but there was no real connection there for her.

He took a bite of his omelet, seeming unperturbed. "Did you take anything?"

She hadn't planned on it, but after seeing the magazines and the state of her old bedroom, she felt she needed something of Ma's. It's not like their relationship was magically healed because of what Frankie had discovered, but she didn't want to delete the memories of her mother like she would a blurry photo, either. "I took a couple of photos and a bracelet." She'd gotten rid of the magazines, though. The fact that she'd found them was a melancholy-tinged spark of sunshine, but the magazines themselves weren't precious.

She waited to see if he'd comment on Ma's magazine collection or Frankie's bedroom, but he didn't say anything. He hummed in affirmation and kept eating. Sitting back in the booth, she crossed her arms and stared at him. He looked up at her, his mouth full. "What?" he said.

There was no point beating around the bush. "Did you know that Ma was collecting *National Geographic* magazines?"

Wing Keung dropped his eyes to his plate and stopped chewing for a moment. It was a short moment, but Frankie noticed.

"And did you know that she hadn't changed my bedroom at all? All the photos were still on the walls, my quilt was still on the bed, even my clothes were still in the drawers."

Her brother continued to avoid her gaze. He shoved another bite in his mouth and shrugged.

"Wing Keung." Her tone was sharp, and if gazes could cut, she was sure that hers would. "Why didn't you tell me?" Despite the tears pressing up behind her eyes, she kept her voice steady. She would not cry again, not in front of her brother. She'd already cried twice in front of Dylan.

He put down his cutlery and tipped his head back, his eyes

sliding past her to the ceiling. He pinched the bridge of his nose. "I didn't want to get in the middle of it," he said. "I told Ma many times that she should reach out to you. Write you a letter or phone you or even send you an email. I told her I would help her. She said it wasn't my job to repair what was broken."

Frankie pursed her lips. "But if I had known that she cared . . . Maybe I would have come back." She couldn't know for sure since it hadn't happened, but maybe she would have come back to town sooner. She could have been there when Ma got sick, although the thought of keeping her company at the hospital seemed out of the question.

Wing Keung shrugged again. "I'm sorry. Ma said that if you wanted to fix things, you would."

"*I* would fix things?" Frankie's anger at her mother resurfaced with a vengeance. "She's the one who told me I was no longer part of the family!" A customer at the table next to them glanced over, so Frankie lowered her voice. "She told me to leave. She's the reason I haven't been back here in fifty years." She glared at her brother as if this were all his fault.

Wing Keung picked up his fork again and took another bite of his omelet. She fumed while he finished chewing, then he said, "Don't you think that's why she didn't contact you?"

Frankie's anger simmered down until it was just under the surface. "What do you mean?"

"She couldn't accept you. She disowned her own daughter, and you know how much family meant to her. She was a proud woman, Frankie. What if she thought you wouldn't want her apology? What if she thought you would rather never see her again after what she did?"

Leaning forward, Frankie put her face in her hands. That made sense. She hated that Wing Keung was probably right and that she hadn't considered that perspective before. But it also wasn't *her* responsibility to make amends.

"Ma wasn't perfect," her brother said, his plate now clean. "I think she was too scared to say anything to you."

So, they'd stayed separated. Ma loving Frankie from a distance, following her career and keeping her bedroom ready for her return. And Frankie feeling bitter and resentful about Ma, not understanding what could push a mother to treat her daughter the way Ma had treated Frankie.

"This is a mess," Frankie said, shaking her head.

"But at least you know the truth now, right?"

She wanted to be angry at Wing Keung for keeping information from her, but he had been respecting Ma's wishes. He had been letting the two of them work it out—if they wanted to. And, in the end, he'd been the reason that Frankie had discovered any of this. She supposed she should be grateful for that, but she needed to stew on it more.

Wing Keung offered to drive her to Ma's place after breakfast, but she insisted on walking. The fresh air would do her good, and the walk would give her time to reflect.

He was waiting by the door when she got there, and she helped him carry the boxes to the car. The house was empty now, other than the furniture. It wouldn't take long to clean that out, especially if she accepted help from all the friends she was unintentionally making while she was in town. Dylan, Evvie, Olivia, Dean, Jamie, Gem, Margie . . . the more she got out on Main Street, the longer that list became.

As Wing Keung drove off, she locked up and stood on the front sidewalk, looking the house over. It was a familiar building, but it was no longer Ma's home. It was empty, and there was nothing left there for Frankie.

As soon as the house was sold and Pumpkin Days was over, there would be nothing left in Juniper Creek for her. She'd go to her cottage in France, drink wine, eat fresh bread and cheese from the market, and take photos at her leisure. The thought of a relaxing retired life should have filled her with excitement.

But all she could think about was a certain plaid-wearing, stormy-eyed librarian.

CHAPTER TWENTY

DYLAN

At seven o'clock on Monday, Dylan pulled up outside the Bluebell. She yawned and shook her head to try and wake herself up. She'd had a late night on Sunday celebrating the success of the raffle with Evvie, Minnie, and Eleanor. In only one day of Pumpkin Days, they'd raised just over a quarter of their goal. With two fundraising events left and the Finale being the biggest one, things were looking up. And she'd had too much wine to celebrate.

Why did Frankie want to leave so fucking early? Dylan would have to walk the dogs later now, but she suspected she wouldn't have the energy when they got back. Putting together the ad copy and submitting it for the online newspaper was going to be a slog as well. Whatever Frankie had in mind for the day, it better not be a big hike.

The front door to the B&B opened before Dylan got there, revealing Frankie in long cargo pants and a black sweater, a camera bag hanging from her shoulder and a cooler at her feet. "I saw you through the window," she said in greeting.

Dylan grunted in response, grabbed the cooler, and turned around, counting on Frankie to follow her to the truck.

"Someone's cheerful this morning," Frankie said, a laugh in her voice. "Too early for you?"

After putting the cooler on the back seat, Dylan hopped in front and waited for Frankie to get in as well. When they were both settled, she said, "Too early and not enough sleep. Didn't even get the dogs out for a walk. Oh—one second." She pulled out her phone and texted Evvie, asking her to take the dogs for a walk for her since Evvie had the day off.

Part of Dylan felt guilty for going out with Frankie on Evvie's day off, especially since Evvie had worked six days in a row. But Evvie had pushed her to go, and Dylan would meet up with her later that day anyway. At dinner the previous night, she'd said, "You'll regret it if you don't." Then, of course, Dylan had to explain what was going on to Minnie and Eleanor. She'd left out the part about necking with Frankie in her childhood bedroom.

"Okay," Dylan said when she was done texting. "Where are we going?"

Frankie pulled out her own phone. "Have you ever been to the Cheam Lake Wetlands Regional Park?"

"No, but I know where it is." Dylan breathed a sigh of relief as she started driving. From what friends had told her in the past, the wetlands were an easy walk with benches to stop at if needed. Dylan's jeans, plaid shirt, jacket, and sneakers were suitable for light walking.

"Perfect. That's where we're going. Also, I brought lunch."

"Figured. Thanks." The thought of eating a picnic lunch with Frankie perked her up a bit. This outing felt increasingly like a date, even if neither of them had called it that. And even if Frankie had yet to tell Dylan if that kiss meant anything.

"I borrowed the cooler from Olivia, and Dean made us sandwiches."

"That's nice of him." She glanced at Frankie out of the corner of her eye. "Making friends, are we?"

Frankie didn't answer for a moment, which was puzzling. That was a straight-forward question, wasn't it? "Summer of '69" played softly on the car radio. Finally, Frankie said, "I wasn't intending to. But I think it's hard not to make friends after spending two weeks in a place."

Dylan glanced at her again. "I bet you have friends all over the world then, with all that traveling." It was difficult to judge from such a quick look, but Dylan swore Frankie frowned.

"Yes, I have quite a few friends." A note of sadness colored Frankie's words.

The two of them were quiet for a few minutes, and Bryan Adams switched to Bon Jovi on the radio. When it was clear Frankie wasn't going to elaborate, Dylan said, "I feel like I'm missing something. Why do you sound upset about having friends?"

Frankie laughed softly and adjusted her camera bag, which she'd put by her feet. "I'm not upset about it. It's nice to have friends, especially when you travel. But I miss them. I haven't seen some of them in years." She was quiet for a moment then continued, "We always said we'd visit each other, but it never seems to happen."

That made sense. It also made Dylan think about the long stretch of time when she hadn't seen Frankie. Had Frankie missed her? Had she thought about Dylan as much as Dylan had thought about her? Almost without thinking, Dylan reached back and touched her own shoulder where her crane tattoo was.

"Sorry," she said.

Frankie shrugged. "It's alright. That's life, isn't it? You build relationships, and then people move on." The weight of those words settled in the truck, and neither of them said anything else until Dylan felt the need to break the silence.

"Want to hear something good?" she said.

Twisting slightly in her seat, Frankie raised an eyebrow at Dylan. "Yes?"

The excitement from the previous night washed over Dylan. "The raffle was more than a success. We're a quarter of the way to our goal."

"Really? That's fantastic, Dylan! Congratulations."

Out of the corner of her eye, Dylan saw a grin taking over Frankie's face. The expression was a relief after Frankie's sadness when she talked about the friends she hadn't seen.

They pulled into the wetlands parking lot, where they were currently the only people in sight.

"Well, that's a good omen for the day," Frankie said. "We can leave the cooler here, I think. The important thing is to get out there while the birds are active. According to the website, the trail only takes an hour to walk. So we'll give it three just to be safe."

"Three?" Dylan's disbelief was involuntary. What was she supposed to do for two extra hours while Frankie took photos?

"Just to be safe," Frankie repeated, an eyebrow raised. She was getting her camera together, adjusting settings and pulling pieces of equipment out of her bag that Dylan didn't recognize. "You could stay with the truck if you want. Or sit on one of the benches. Did you bring a book?"

Dylan felt exposed. Of course she had brought a book. Her current read, *Beach Read* by Emily Henry, was on the back seat. And she always had a mass-market paperback copy of *Pride and Prejudice* in her glove box just in case. You never knew when you'd get a moment to read, or when you'd finish a book and not have another one on hand.

"I'm coming with you," she said, her tone leaving no room for argument.

Frankie grinned as if she knew all along that Dylan would say that.

Rolling her eyes, Dylan followed Frankie to the start of a gravel trail. As they walked, a peacefulness enveloped them along with the trickling of the stream and a few bird calls. In the chill of the morning, Dylan *almost* saw the appeal of coming out here this early. With no other people around, it felt as if they were part of nature rather than tourists or intruders.

They walked over a couple of floating bridges and onto a

raised viewing platform. The landscape was lush with greenery, small ripples creating a mesmerizing effect on the water.

"Do you see that?" Frankie said, bringing her camera up to her eye, training it on something at the water's edge among the plants.

"What?" Dylan matched her volume to Frankie's hushed words, and her heartbeat sped up even though she had no idea what she was looking for. Something alive, presumably.

"A green heron," Frankie said, her shutter clicking. "It's dark, with blueish-green feathers. Shorter than what you're probably thinking of."

Dylan moved closer to Frankie to better see what she was seeing. Something moved and resolved itself into the shape of a bird. "It's ugly," Dylan said.

Frankie laughed through her nose. "Okay, it's not the prettiest bird I've ever seen. But I wouldn't call it *ugly* either."

After a couple minutes, Frankie was ready to move on. The trail continued along a stream, and trees stretched up over their heads, casting shadows over them. Dylan zipped her jacket closed, the cool air waking her up more. The trail split, and they took the left side, but it eventually all looped together.

As they walked, Frankie stopped a few times to take more photos. She pointed out her subjects to Dylan. "This is a sora," she said, pointing out a squat bird with a bright yellow beak. "I'm happy it's still here. They fly down to Central and South America in the fall."

"On those tiny wings?"

Frankie smiled. "Yes, on those tiny wings."

They also saw a northern harrier flying overhead, and a sharp-shinned hawk eyed them from high in a tree. Frankie showed Dylan the photos she caught of each of them, and Dylan marveled at the clarity and sharpness of the images. She'd seen Frankie's work, but it was different to see her in action.

"Why haven't I seen these birds before?" Dylan asked. This place wasn't even an hour from Juniper Creek, and yet she'd never been here. She'd never felt any interest in looking at birds, but watching Frankie's face light up when she spotted a bird made Dylan excited to see them too.

Continuing around another path brought them to a variation of the landscape, and they saw even more birds on that side of the wetlands. Many times, they heard a bird before they saw it, or they heard it and never saw it at all.

In contrast to her expectations, Dylan wasn't bored as Frankie stopped to take photos. While Frankie watched the birds, Dylan watched Frankie. Her passion was clear in her voice as she explained what she was doing and what plants and animals surrounded them, but it was also evident in her posture and how she moved. Her movements became smoother somehow, and she breathed deeply and slowly as she looked through her viewfinder, almost like she was a predator stalking her prey. But then she'd smile in satisfaction, her eyes crinkling at the corners, and Dylan couldn't help but smile with her.

"I think I've got plenty to work with," Frankie said, looking at her watch. "And it's only ten. That didn't take as long as I expected."

Dylan blinked and felt like she was coming out of a trance. How was it ten already? The last couple of hours had flown by, and she wasn't even tired anymore.

"It's not quite lunchtime, but are you interested in eating?" Frankie asked.

Dylan's stomach rumbled. "Does that answer your question?" Until that moment, she hadn't even realized she was hungry.

As they walked back to the truck, Frankie kept her camera out. "You never know when something will fly past or show up in the water," she said.

There were a few more cars in the parking lot now, and a couple waved at them as they walked in the opposite direction. When they arrived at the truck, Dylan pulled out the cooler.

"Ha, you *did* bring a book," Frankie said from behind her. She must have spotted *Beach Read*. "Did you expect to be bored?"

Dylan shot her a look. "Not really. I always bring a book with me. Would I be a proper librarian otherwise?"

"Maybe not."

They walked side by side to the picnic area near the parking lot. Dylan had the urge to grab Frankie's hand with her free one, but Frankie still hadn't said anything about what she wanted. And Dylan wasn't sure what she herself wanted either. If she let Frankie in, she was also inviting the opportunity for heartbreak.

One of the picnic tables was occupied by a family, a little girl of maybe five or six eating crackers while one of her parents texted on their phone and the other petted a shaggy dog. "Nice morning," the person with the dog said as Frankie and Dylan passed them.

"Very," Frankie replied, leading Dylan to the nearest empty table.

Dylan set down the cooler and opened the top to reveal a container with two sandwiches, two bottles of water, two oranges, and a large slice of cake. "You brought cake?"

"What?" Frankie peered into the cooler. "Dean must have put that there. I did not ask for cake. It looks good, though."

"It sure does. Chocolate is my favorite."

"Really?" Frankie tilted her head at Dylan. "Carrot cake used to be your favorite."

Dylan shrugged, a bit irked at the reminder of the distance between them. Frankie no longer knew what her favorite cake was, and she no longer knew many things about Frankie. "Carrot is still good, but chocolate is the best."

The two of them sat on opposite sides of the table and Frankie pulled everything out, placing one of each item in front of Dylan and one in front of herself. There was only a single container of cake, which she put between them, setting two forks on top. "I guess we're sharing."

Dylan dug into her sandwich. They ate in companionable silence for a few minutes, until Frankie began peeling her orange and said, "So, I was thinking."

"Careful," Dylan said. "I've heard that can be dangerous."

Frankie snorted. "Very funny." She popped a section of orange into her mouth. "I was thinking about . . . the other day."

Dylan sat up straighter. "The other day . . . ?"

"At Ma's. What we did . . ." She looked at her as if Dylan might have forgotten. As if she could possibly forget the feeling of Frankie's lips on hers. The fire she had felt under her skin when Frankie skimmed her fingers up Dylan's sides.

"Mm-hmm," Dylan said, not trusting herself to say more. She didn't want to throw off whatever Frankie was getting at.

Frankie continued, "I'm leaving in a couple weeks. You know that."

"I do." Christ, she was taking a long time to get to the point.

"But as much as I didn't want it to . . . that day meant something to me. What we did . . . that meant something to me."

Dylan's pulse pounded in her ears and she squirmed, trying to make herself sit still while Frankie kept talking even though all she wanted to do was take Frankie's face between her palms and kiss her until she couldn't think.

"Dylan, you were my first love." Dylan inhaled sharply and her breathing sped up. "I don't know if you know that, but you were. When you told me you were engaged . . . I couldn't handle it. I didn't know what to do with myself, with that news. I didn't think I could be your best friend and see you with someone else." Frankie looked away from Dylan and down at the table.

"Hey," Dylan said, waiting until Frankie looked up at her again. It was as if gravity had shifted and her body was ten times lighter. Frankie had loved her. "I didn't know that for sure, but I suspected that's what happened. I didn't know until I was in my forties that I felt the same way." Frankie's eyes widened. "About women, in general. And about you."

Frankie's lips parted the slightest bit, and Dylan wanted to touch them so much, her heart ached.

"Wing Keung had hinted at that, but I wasn't sure." Frankie's forehead creased as she frowned.

Dylan lowered her voice. "It took me longer to come to terms with everything. You've always been more free-spirited than me. You've known yourself better—who you are and what you want. Look at the career you made!"

Frankie grinned sheepishly. "Your career is pretty impressive too."

"Yeah, well," Dylan waved her off. Her career hadn't been born from ambition; it had risen from her attachment to the library because of Frankie. "So . . . where do we go from here?" That was the burning question. Their feelings were out in the open now, but what would they do with them?

"If we decide to . . . be together," Frankie said, "it can only be until I leave. I don't want to have a long-distance relationship. I care about you, Dylan. But you've got the library and your family. And I've got my cottage in France."

Dylan licked her lips. She wanted to tell Frankie to forget France and stay in Juniper Creek. But this was Frankie's decision. Dylan wanted to be with her while she could, even if it meant leaving herself exposed to emotional damage. The fact that their time together would be short was almost better; at least this time, she was prepared for Frankie to leave. "I *might* have the library," she said.

With narrowed eyes, Frankie said, "You *will* have it. You said yourself that the raffle was more than successful. I don't think we've got anything to worry about."

They stared at each other for a beat, and something passed between them in that moment that filled Dylan with a shiver of anticipation.

"Okay," she said.

"Okay?"

Dylan held out her hands on the tabletop, palms up, and Frankie cautiously grabbed them. Her palms were sweaty, but Dylan didn't mind. "If that's what you want—us being together until you leave—then I'm okay with that." Saying it out loud made it feel truer.

"Alright."

The two of them sat there, the air between them crackling, and it was a bit awkward since the family was still sitting at the other table. Frankie rubbed her thumbs back and forth across the insides of Dylan's wrists, and Dylan shifted on the bench. Apparently, she could still feel some things as strongly as she did when she was younger.

Finally, she couldn't take it anymore. This was a public space, for fuck's sake. If Frankie wanted to keep touching her like that, they needed to move somewhere private.

"Want cake?" she said, pulling her hands out from underneath Frankie's.

They opened the container of cake and each took a bite. The cake was moist and fudgy, and Dylan had the urge to moan as she swallowed. Although that might not have been just from the cake.

Even if whatever they had ended when Frankie left again, Dylan would savor what she could get. She wouldn't be caught off guard, and she knew not to let herself get too deep into . . . whatever this was.

But not letting herself get too deep was never as easy as it sounded.

Dear Library Board,

My name is Hugo, and I am one of the assistant librarians at the Juniper Creek Library. I'll be honest with you—I don't know where I'd be if not for the library. I discovered who I was here.

I had never felt like I fit in my body. I didn't like the clothes my parents dressed me in when I was a kid or the toys they told me I should play with. I wanted short hair instead of long hair, and I wanted to play basketball, not be in ballet. I wanted to hang out with the guys at school, and I never understood what the girls in my class meant when they talked about having crushes.

It wasn't until I found a book at the library about a trans woman that I realized I was trans. I did more research and talked to my parents about it, and it was like everything clicked into place for them as well as for me.

I'm sure I would have discovered the queer community without the library eventually, but the library helped me figure out who I was and who I wanted to be. Now I have a job here, and I wouldn't give it up for anything.

Thanks,
Hugo Willingham

CHAPTER TWENTY-ONE

FRANKIE

The ride home from the wetlands was charged in a completely different way than the ride there, as if a new awareness had settled over Frankie's skin.

She rested her hand on Dylan's thigh the whole way home, amazed at how easy it was to touch Dylan when she gave herself permission to—and when Dylan wanted her to.

What was Dylan to her now? Her new lover? Her temporary partner? It was probably better not to put a label on whatever they had, especially since it was going to last only a couple of weeks.

When Dylan dropped her off at the Bluebell again, she leaned over for a kiss. Dylan slid her hand into Frankie's hair, and Frankie leaned into her as their lips touched. This kiss was soft, delicate, and Dylan tasted like chocolate. It was better than any dessert Frankie had ever tried.

Frankie squeezed Dylan's thigh, feeling embarrassingly feral. "I'm going to come into the library tomorrow to work on the photos," she said, more breathless than she expected. She wished she could spend the rest of the day with Dylan, but Dylan already had plans with Evvie.

Dylan smiled, her eyes practically glittering. "I look forward to seeing you there."

It was difficult for Frankie to focus on anything at all for the rest of the day. She picked up one of the romance novels Olivia had recommended and tried to read in the Bluebell's back garden, but she found herself reading the same passage over and over again.

Eventually, she headed to Ma's house to look over what needed to be done. Dylan had given her the number for two construction workers in town: Gerard and Landon, a father and son duo. They were related to Leah, who ran the bookstore; Juniper Creek may have changed, but it seemed like everyone was still connected. Frankie planned to call them this week to see if they could give her a quote on repairs. She didn't want to do any major renovations—just enough to make the house sellable.

The house felt so impersonal now that it was empty. The memories that had swarmed her on her first visit were still there, but they were in the back of her mind. They had quieted down now that there wasn't as much left to draw them out. It was a relief, and it would be easier for Frankie to let go of the house now. To let go of Juniper Creek.

To let go of Dylan.

That thought made her halt in her tracks, like she'd hit an invisible barrier. Letting go of Dylan wasn't something she wanted to think about. She had two weeks left to enjoy the relationship she had let go of before. She would be able to let go of it again. She had to.

It was better that way.

~

AT THE LIBRARY the next day, Frankie made herself comfortable at a table so she could edit her photos. Shortly after she sat down, Dylan came over and greeted her with a kiss, only stopping when they heard a kid whisper loudly, "Mom, why are those ladies kissing?"

When Dylan pulled away, Frankie saw a little girl duck behind a nearby shelf. Dylan and Frankie locked eyes and burst into laughter, and the girl ran off giggling as her mother shook her head, smiling.

"It's wild to me that we can do that here," Frankie said, feeling so giddy that it was difficult to sit still. "I can't imagine people being happy with us kissing in public when I lived here." She thought of the horrified expression on her mother's face when she told her that she loved Dylan. Not like a sister, and not like a best friend either.

"It took a few decades," Dylan said, rolling her eyes. "Some people still aren't okay with it, but I think they're in the minority. At least, they're not as vocal as they used to be."

Frankie nodded. In her travels, she'd been to places where being gay was completely normal; it had been refreshing the first time a woman had asked her on a date openly, instead of through code of some sort. She'd also been to places that condemned homosexuality, though, and she knew what it meant to fear anyone finding out who she was. Even in countries that claimed to be queer friendly, being yourself could get you in trouble. A few areas of the world made the Juniper Creek of her childhood look like paradise.

"Anyway," Dylan said, waving a hand. "Would you like to go for dinner tonight? There's a bistro in Abbotsford that Evvie keeps telling me I should try. We could go there?"

"Sure." Frankie's cheeks warmed, just a little bit. She was going on a *date* again. With Dylan.

The rest of that day flew by. Frankie went back to the Bluebell for a quick nap and to get ready for dinner. She'd never really worn makeup besides the occasional lipstick, but she smoothed out her hair, pulled a couple of chin hairs, and wore the nicest shirt she had with her.

Dylan was running her hands through her hair as Frankie got into the passenger seat. "Is everything alright?"

Dylan grimaced. "Maybe. I realized when I opened my email this afternoon that I forgot to send in an ad for the online newspaper. It's not something we usually do for Pumpkin Days, but I thought it could give us a boost this year. I guess I forgot after the wetlands and . . . everything else." One side of her mouth twitched up slightly.

Frankie ran a hand lightly down Dylan's arm and grinned when Dylan bit her lip in response. "I'm sure it will be fine. Hugo already has social media ads running, right?" Dylan nodded. "Good. Then forget about it for tonight and enjoy dinner. With me."

After that, Dylan seemed to relax. On the drive to the bistro, she put on "Wild One" by Bobby Rydell and "I Got You Babe" by Sonny and Cher, and Frankie laughed harder than she'd laughed in ages. The food at the restaurant was delicious, and they shared another slice of chocolate cake for dessert.

When Dylan dropped her off afterward, Frankie was tempted to grab Dylan's jacket collar and pull her inside, but that felt too indulgent. This wasn't serious. It wasn't going to last. She agreed to go to Dylan's house the next night, though. To spend time with her dogs, of course.

Dylan's house looked about how she expected: light colors on the walls, dark bookshelves stuffed full of books, plaid throw pillows, and a well-worn hardwood floor. An embroidered tapestry hung on the wall beside the TV, displaying the quote, "Angry people are not always wise" surrounded by blue and yellow flowers.

"Is that from *Pride and Prejudice*?" Frankie asked, gesturing to it as Dylan brought her a glass of wine.

Dylan smiled and her gaze softened. "Yeah. Evvie made that for me when she was in her needlework phase—she's got a new hobby every few months. She picked that quote because I had been complaining about a particularly stubborn library patron who insisted he knew how to do my job better than I did."

Frankie sipped her wine and nodded in approval. "That seems fitting." She was curled up on Dylan's couch with Bingley sitting by her feet, and she wiggled her toes until they were under Bingley's warm furry body. "So you leaned into your love for *Pride and Prejudice*, clearly."

Darcy put her head on Dylan's lap, looking up at her with wide eyes until Dylan bent down to kiss her head. "I don't think I ever leaned *out* of it," she said, and Frankie laughed.

"Well, the names fit your dogs. We should do a fall photoshoot with them!"

Dylan rolled up the sleeves of her plaid shirt and adjusted her leg so she slid closer to Frankie. "Why?"

"So you can put cute photos of them on the wall? Or maybe people would buy them at the market."

"My dogs are cute, but I don't think they're *that* cute," Dylan said, laughing.

They watched *Pride and Prejudice* after that, of course—the 2005 version—and Frankie almost told Dylan about the beat-up paperback in her suitcase. About how she'd had a copy of the book with her wherever she went.

For the longest time, she told herself it was because the book was nostalgic for her. It held good memories, and she enjoyed the story. But she'd always known it was more than that. Having the book with her felt like holding on to a piece of Dylan. She hadn't fully let go, no matter what she liked to tell herself.

Watching Dylan's face as Darcy and Elizabeth walked toward each other across a field made Frankie's heart soar. Dylan had tears in her eyes, just enough that Frankie could see the water glistening in the reflection from the television. She clearly still loved the story as much as she had when they were younger.

Reaching over, Frankie laced her fingers with Dylan's. Dylan leaned her head on Frankie's shoulder, and Frankie never wanted to move from that spot for the rest of her life.

~

ON FRIDAY, Dylan's next day off, the two of them went for brunch at the diner, then they met Gerard and Landon at Ma's house. The four of them did a sweep of the property, taking note of everything that needed doing. Frankie had made a list on Monday, but Gerard pointed out things she had missed.

He smoothed his mustache as he stood with his arms crossed. "You're leaving at the end of the month? We might be able to finish it all by then if we start right away, but I make no guarantees. That only gives us eleven days, if I'm counting correctly."

The reminder of how much time she had left in town sent a spike of panic through Frankie. Less than two weeks didn't seem like enough time to get the house finished. It didn't seem like enough time for a lot of things.

Landon nodded. "I think there's a good chance we can do it. This is our slow season, so I can spend most of the next week here."

"Perfect, thank you so much," Frankie said. "I suppose you could keep working on it even when I'm not here." She could get Wing Keung to manage any in-person tasks for her, Dylan would be there to help, and Frankie could liaise with a realtor from France if she had to. But extending her stay was starting to seem like a better idea, for more than one reason.

Gerard offered to store the remaining furniture in his trailer until Frankie knew what to do with it, and she took him up on the offer.

"Want to come over to my house?" Dylan asked as they left Ma's place.

Frankie intertwined her fingers with Dylan's, and a pleasant warmth traveled up her arm. "Yes. I can show you how the photos from Monday turned out."

They stopped by the Bluebell so Frankie could pick up her laptop. At Dylan's house, she made herself comfortable on the couch, Darcy asleep by her feet while Bingley snored on the love seat. It was pleasantly domestic.

Dylan tucked herself into Frankie's side as she started up her editing program and pulled up the photos she'd worked on.

"They're as gorgeous as I knew they'd be," Dylan said. "I think these will sell for a lot. You're sure you don't want to keep any of the profits?"

"I don't need it," Frankie said. "I want to give it all to the library."

Dylan kissed her full on the mouth, but before they really got into things, Dylan gently pushed Frankie away with the excuse of wanting to look at the photos more closely.

It shouldn't have been a big deal, but Frankie felt the bite of rejection anyway. On Monday when Dylan had agreed to be with her until she left, she had seemed so happy. But there was clearly still a distance between them that Dylan wasn't ready to close, and Frankie needed to be okay with that.

In fact, it was probably healthier to keep that distance there. The closer Frankie got to Dylan, the higher the chances that something would go wrong.

CHAPTER TWENTY-TWO

DYLAN

Saturday morning was gray, the sky threatening to pour. The weather had been bright and warm all week, and Dylan had barely worried, even after forgetting to submit the ad. The library already had a good chunk of money from the raffle, and the scavenger hunt was a popular annual activity. But looking at the gloomy sky overhead, she had the sinking feeling that she'd been too optimistic.

She stood at the library window, wishing she could control the weather. When she'd taken the dogs for their walk that morning, she could *feel* the rain in the air. She knew what was going to happen: the town-wide scavenger hunt was going to be a bust.

Jamie came in the front doors, her green raincoat swishing as she walked, a few splashes of water on her shoulders and in her hair.

"It's already raining?" Dylan asked. She could hear the despair in her own voice.

Her mouth pressed into a grim line, Jamie nodded. "We've got the tents set up out front, and I'm bringing over hot chocolate, tea, and coffee. We'll sell them at a dollar per cup. The Dawoods made a bunch of cookies too, so that should help."

"If there's even anyone to sell them to," Dylan grumbled.

"The scavenger hunt doesn't start until one," Jamie said. "People will show up, you'll see." Her words lacked conviction, which didn't make Dylan feel any better.

Evvie bustled through the front doors, closing a rainbow umbrella. She wore a classic bright yellow raincoat and matching rainboots.

"Ev," Dylan said. "I thought you were working today."

"I was, but it was slow. A few clients called to cancel their appointments because of the rain. And we only have one doctor in today, anyway." People were canceling vet appointments? That didn't bode well. When Evvie saw the look on Dylan's face, she added, "I don't think the rain will be that bad."

But it was.

As Dylan, Evvie, and Frankie sat in The June Bug for lunch, rain hammered on the roof. The three of them were silent, and Frankie reached to hold Dylan's hand in the booth between them. The contact was soothing, but only a little. If people didn't show up for the scavenger hunt, the library would miss out on a large portion of their predicted funds.

After lunch, the three of them settled at the tables under the tents set up in the library parking lot. Dylan and Frankie were going to sell drinks while Evvie handed out cookies. Lorelai, Iris, and Hijiri stood at the library doors, prepared to hand out scavenger hunt maps and answer questions.

Usually, at that point in the day, there'd be a crowd waiting for the scavenger hunt to kick off. But the only other people in the parking lot were two ladies there to use the library, Lorelai's husband and son, Charlie and Kat, Minnie and Eleanor, and a handful of locals with their kids. It was more like a short lineup than a crowd.

Damn it all to hell. Dylan was not a crier, but a lump had formed in her throat. She leaned over until her shoulder touched Frankie's.

"What are we going to do?" she whispered.

She thought people cared about the library, but they clearly didn't care enough to brave the fucking rain. And if they didn't care enough on one day of bad weather, did the library have any chance of staying open?

As the afternoon went on, a few more people showed up. The volunteers sold drinks and cookies, and they even emptied the hot chocolate and had to call Jamie for a refill, but it wasn't enough.

Dylan could barely bring herself to speak as they handed out drinks. She shifted from foot to foot as she stood waiting, and whenever there was a lull, she ran into the library to check her email or find a different task to occupy her thoughts. If she stood there for too long, staring out at the mostly empty parking lot, she was going to scream.

It was cold enough that Hugo had brought in a portable heater for them, and Evvie was huddled up in front of it, her rainbow scarf around her neck and a blue toque on her head. At the look on Evvie's face, the tiny spark of hope Dylan clung to vanished altogether. Evvie was sometimes so bubbly that she annoyed Dylan—but today, she was subdued, her face falling as soon as the scavenger hunt participants walked away with their drinks, maps, and cookies.

At five o'clock, they wrapped up for the day and huddled inside the library as Iris counted the money they'd collected. "Just under $150," she said, her expression apologetic.

Dylan ran her hands through her hair, and Frankie reached over to rub her back. "$150," Dylan said. "That's *jack shit*."

"These things happen," Lorelai said. "The scavenger hunt tends to be the least busy of the Pumpkin Days events every year. Next Saturday, we'll see a much bigger turnout."

Gwen chewed on her nails, and she appeared extra small in her oversized black jacket. "But will it be enough?" she asked.

"It has to be," Evvie said, looking around at them all. "We have to make it enough. If we don't, the library closes."

A muscle twitched in Dylan's jaw, and she walked off toward her office, barely taking in her surroundings as she went.

How could they have made so little money? Christ, that was

probably a record low for the scavenger hunt event, and this was the year they needed a record high.

Dylan slammed her office door and sank into her chair, groaning as she collapsed forward.

She should have done more. For the past week, she'd been so caught up in spending time with Frankie that she hadn't put much effort at all into marketing the scavenger hunt or coming up with ideas to make it more successful. She'd missed the deadline on that ad, and getting that in could have made all the difference.

This is why she didn't do things for herself—every time she did, something bad happened.

As much as she wanted to be with Frankie, to catch up on all the years they had been apart, to feel that rush she got when she was with her, to feel her body come alive again like it hadn't in years . . . it was distracting her.

The library was her life. Her entire fucking world revolved around this building, this job, this community. There was only one event left in Pumpkin Days now, and they only had a week to get everything ready for it. She couldn't afford to let anything distract her.

Including Frankie.

Dear Library Board,

As the mayor of Juniper Creek, I have a different perspective of what happens in and around town. I see what people need, and I hear both their praise and their complaints. I have only ever heard praise about the library, and I can verify from my own experience that it's a bright spot in this town.

My son, Jesse, loves going to the library every Saturday. We go there for story time, and he picks out his own books for us to check out. I can't imagine raising him in a town without a place that champions literacy and free learning. I want him to have access to library services wherever he goes, even in small towns like ours.

As good neighbors, it's our responsibility to see what is needed in our communities and to fulfill those needs. We need our library.

Yálh yuxw kw'as hó:y (Thank you),
Lorelai Akan
Mayor of Juniper Creek

CHAPTER TWENTY-THREE

FRANKIE

Frankie needed time to think that evening after the disappointing turnout for the scavenger hunt, so she ordered in Chinese food to her room at the Bluebell. It was very much Canadian Chinese food, not the food she had eaten growing up, but it wasn't bad. Sometimes she wanted something deep-fried, even if it would give her hot air.

She sat at the small side table by the window. Raindrops clung to the glass and the sky was gray, fitting her mood. In the Bluebell's small backyard, a pergola provided shade for a seating area right outside the patio doors. Frankie had been out there a few times; the patio chairs were cushioned and surprisingly comfy.

Frankie bit into a piece of ginger beef and let her gaze go unfocused. How were they going to make up for the funds they had missed today? What they really needed was to find someone with money who would be willing to donate a large portion of it to the library. But there weren't many rich people in Juniper Creek; most people who lived here had grown up in the area or had family here, and they weren't exactly wealthy. Either that, or they'd moved to town to open a small business, and small businesses were not known for being lucrative.

Wing Keung might have donated money if she asked. But he

wasn't exactly rich either, and he had his family to look after. It wasn't often that she regretted donating much of her income over the years to wildlife conservation efforts, but it would have been nice to have more cash on hand right about now. Ma's house would probably sell for a good amount, but she was unlikely to fix it up and sell it before the end of the month.

Selling Ma's furniture was the only useful thing she could think of to do. She would sell the furniture online and donate the profit to the library. She phoned Gerard, and he agreed to send her photos of each piece of furniture so she could post them. With that done, she had nothing to do but sit and wallow.

She thought about her cottage in France. If she had flown back there after the funeral, she wouldn't be in this mess. Her heart wouldn't be aching at the thought of the library closing, and she wouldn't be remembering Dylan's pained expression as Iris announced the pitiful amount they had raised today.

The urge to reach out to Dylan, to draw her into her arms, had been almost overwhelming. But whatever was between them had felt fragile in that moment, like ice in the spring.

She put her elbow in something sticky from one of the many takeout dishes and sighed, wiping it off with a napkin.

As much as she wanted to go back to France and put her feet up, she was happy here. If she had left and let Wing Keung take over the house, she never would have found out that Ma had been thinking about her after all. Sure, it had been painful, but her memories of Ma had a lighter tinge to them now. The edges of the wound she bore throughout life were healing, if only a little bit.

When she finished her meal, she reached for the fortune cookie. She didn't believe in fortunes, exactly, but a positive message wouldn't hurt.

Love is the only true adventure.

She read the paper twice, thinking about Dylan and the battered copy of *Pride and Prejudice* in her suitcase. The fortune seemed more like a reflection of what had already happened rather than a prediction, although she wouldn't call what she had with Dylan now *love*, even if that was what she yearned for.

Laughing at herself, she got up and pulled out the book from under one of her shirts, sliding the fortune into the front cover. She was seventy-three years old, finally connecting with the woman she had loved her whole life. With a woman she had history with, whose dreams she was trying to help save. And she was leaving in a little over a week. What had she gotten herself into?

ON SUNDAY MORNING, Frankie woke up with a sense of purpose. She didn't have any concrete plans for the day, but she needed to talk to Dylan. Everything had felt untethered after the scavenger hunt, and Dylan had needed time to process what had happened. But today was a new day, and Frankie was going to make it a good one. For herself and for Dylan.

Dean made her pancakes, which she ate with fresh fruit, and Olivia told her a bit about her latest romance read. Then Frankie stopped by the library just in case Dylan had come in already; she wasn't scheduled to work until noon, but she seemed to be there all the time anyway.

"Nope, she hasn't come in yet," Hugo said when Frankie asked. He frowned. "I think she needed time away after yesterday."

"Alright. Thank you." She waved and walked to Dylan's house, glaring up at the sun as she did so. Why couldn't it have been this nice out the day before? There was no trace of the downpour, not even a wet patch on the sidewalk or water in the gutters. It was as if it hadn't rained at all.

When Frankie knocked on Dylan's door, there was no answer. She wondered if Dylan was out with Evvie or Minnie and Eleanor, but a cheerful bark drew her attention to the sidewalk behind her.

"Oh, good morning," she said as Dylan walked toward her, pulled along by Darcy and Bingley. "Don't you usually walk the dogs earlier?"

"Yeah," Dylan said, fishing her house key out of her jean pocket. "It's been a slow morning. Want coffee?"

Frankie gently pushed away Darcy and Bingley as Dylan opened the door. "Sure," she said, following her inside. "I've already had one cup, but another wouldn't hurt."

She made herself comfortable at the kitchen table as Dylan brewed a pot of coffee. Neither of them said anything, and yesterday's disappointment hung in the air. Frankie gave the dogs a good scratch behind their ears and Dylan washed a few dishes while the coffee brewed.

Finally, Dylan put a steaming cup in front of Frankie and sat down in the chair next to her with her own mug between her hands.

"So," Frankie started. "Yesterday wasn't fun."

Dylan snorted. "You can say that again."

"I think the library will be okay, though. We've got the market coming up, and we've filled most of the spots. We still have donations trickling in too." Bingley spread out in a dog-shaped puddle at her feet, huffing as she laid her head on the floor.

"I know." Dylan glanced at Frankie then stared into her mug as if it contained something more interesting than bean water. "I keep thinking about what would happen if the library closed. What I would do with myself. This job has been my entire life since the kids moved out."

Frankie looked into her own mug. She knew what it was like to feel so passionate about something—or someone—that you didn't know what you would do without it. But she had survived, mostly by throwing herself into photography and traveling. By losing herself in other people for brief stints and constantly bracing herself for the inevitable heartbreak.

"You could retire?" Frankie said tentatively. She knew about

Evvie's reluctance to retire, but Dylan hadn't expressed her feelings around the subject.

Dylan glanced up at Frankie again, this time with a wry smile on her lips. "I could. But again, what would I do with myself?"

The first words that popped into Frankie's mind were *spend time with me*, but she didn't dare say that. She was leaving, after all. And she didn't expect Dylan to ask her to stay. She didn't even know how she'd react if Dylan *did* ask. Juniper Creek felt more like home now than it had when she was younger—it was more liberal, more accepting, more open—but could she throw away her cottage and her retirement plans for it? For a woman she once loved and had now been semi-dating for only a week?

"You could read all the books you've always wanted to read but haven't gotten to yet," Frankie suggested, feeling lighter when Dylan gave her a genuine grin.

"That idea is almost enough to make me okay with retiring," Dylan said. She sighed. "I suppose I could visit my kids more, and my grandkids. They don't come here as often as I'd like."

The two of them sat in contemplative silence, each of them staring into their mugs.

"What are you thinking about?" Dylan asked, placing her hand gently on Frankie's wrist. "You've got that furrow between your brows that means you're thinking intensely about something."

Frankie took a deep breath and locked eyes with Dylan. "Why does your choice have to be work or your kids? What about choosing something for *you*?"

Dylan took her hand back. She didn't snatch it back—not exactly—but Frankie could tell her words had stung.

"The library *is* for me," Dylan said, crossing her arms.

"Okay, yes, that's not exactly what I meant. What I'm trying to say is that you've made the library your entire life, to the point where you don't know what you'd do without it. There's got to be something else you care about, something you'd enjoy doing."

Frankie didn't know why she was pushing the matter, but it seemed necessary.

Dylan shook her head. "I don't know. The only thing I do outside of work is spend time with my friends and read. That's all I've ever needed."

Frankie winced. Dylan's friends and the library were all she ever needed. She'd never needed Frankie.

She probably hadn't pined like Frankie had or carried around something that reminded her of Frankie. Frankie shook her head at herself, at how ridiculous she was being. People didn't *need* each other.

For a long time, Frankie had thought she needed Dylan to be happy, and that without her, she had no purpose. One of her earliest affirmations had been *I don't need someone else to be happy*. She'd found a purpose, and she'd made it work. Even if the Dylan-shaped hole in her heart had never filled.

"Well, maybe think about it," Frankie said, pushing back her chair. "Thank you for the coffee."

CHAPTER TWENTY-FOUR

DYLAN

"Frankie, wait." Dylan stood and reached for Frankie, gently grabbing her shoulder. "Stay. Please. You have a point."

As much as Dylan didn't want to admit it, Frankie was right. Even when she was married and raising her kids, she'd poured herself into her work. The library was everything to her, and if she lost it, she'd be left floating adrift. And she had no one to blame for that but herself.

She was being a hypocrite, telling Evvie she should retire then pushing back against her own retirement.

"I will figure it out, if the library closes. But I don't want to talk about that right now. Can we change the subject?"

Frankie nodded and turned back to the table, back to her unfinished cup of coffee. The two of them took their seats again.

"So," Frankie started, "what do you want to talk about?"

Dylan did have a question in mind, although it wasn't exactly a lighter subject than the last one. In fact, it might bring up heavier things. But she'd been waiting fifty years to ask it, and she was comfortable enough now to bring it up.

She reached for Frankie's hand. "You don't have to answer this if you don't want to. I've just always wondered . . . Why did you choose to leave that day? What pushed you to just . . . go?"

Frankie swallowed, hard. "That day . . . I was coming to meet you when you opened your front door."

Dylan remembered that. She'd been going to tell Frankie about her engagement, and Frankie had been right there when she opened the door, like she'd known Dylan had news.

"I wanted to tell you . . ." Frankie continued, pulling her hand out of Dylan's and grabbing her own arms, like she was hugging herself. "I'd been trying to work up the courage for a while, but it was hard for me. That day, I was coming to tell you that I liked women. That I liked *you*."

Dylan put her hand over her mouth. She'd figured out that Frankie must have had feelings for her, but Christ . . . she had no idea that Frankie had been coming to tell her in that moment. "Oh." No wonder Dylan's news had sent Frankie fleeing.

"Yeah." Frankie laughed softly. "The irony of the situation hit me later."

Dylan shook her head. "Why didn't you say something to me? I understand being upset, but why did you just leave? For fifty years?" Her throat felt thick. This was confirmation that she'd pushed her best friend away—not just away from her but away from Juniper Creek. And for half a lifetime.

Frankie let out a breath. "Ma."

"Your mom?"

A couple of tears spilled down Frankie's cheeks, and she quickly wiped them away. "I had planned to tell you first because I thought you wouldn't react too badly, if badly at all. Then I was going to tell my family. Or, at least, I would work up to telling them. When you told me you were engaged . . . I don't know what I was thinking. It's like I had finally worked myself up to tell someone, and then I couldn't tell you."

The air in the room suddenly felt too thick for Dylan to breathe. "So you told your mom."

"I told her and Wing Keung at the same time."

"And it didn't go well."

Frankie puffed out her cheeks. "Wing Keung didn't say anything. He took one look at Ma's face and went to his room. I should have followed his lead." She sighed. "Ma told me that I was unnatural. That she wouldn't have someone like me in the family. That I wasn't welcome at her house."

"Oh, Frankie." Dylan reached for Frankie's hands. She knew Frankie's relationship with her mother had been strained, but she'd never known the details. Wing Keung always said it wasn't his business to explain. "No wonder you never came back. I'm so sorry. I wish I had known."

So, it hadn't been entirely her fault. That made her feel slightly better, but Frankie shouldn't have had to go through that.

"I had to leave. I couldn't stay here," Frankie said.

Dylan nodded. She wanted to tell Frankie that she could have stayed, that she and Dylan could have figured out something. But there was no use speculating about what could have been. "I wish I had known. I'm sorry."

Frankie glanced up at Dylan from under her wet lashes. "Why didn't you ever ask Wing Keung for my number? Or send me a letter?"

Dylan had thought about doing that very thing too many times to count, but she couldn't bring herself to, knowing that she'd been left behind. Knowing that she had pushed her best friend away. Everything made more sense now that she knew what Ms. Wong had said, but it still hurt. Especially since Frankie hadn't even told her at the time why she was leaving. Instead of saying that, she asked, "Why didn't you ever call *me* when you knew my number? Or send *me* a letter?"

Frankie pursed her lips for a moment before she answered. "You were getting married, and that hurt. I didn't think I could see you with someone else and be happy for you. It was selfish of me, obviously. I wanted you to pick me, and you didn't. By the time I realized how stupid I was being, it felt too late to call."

Dylan squeezed Frankie's hands, needing to feel the solidity of her. "If you had called, I would have answered. Every time."

There was a pause as the two of them looked at each other. "Would it have changed anything?" Frankie asked.

Dylan frowned. "Maybe? Maybe I would have realized I was gay sooner, but I don't know."

What was there to say now? They had both made their choices, and they couldn't go back and change the past. This wasn't *Outlander*.

"I wish things had been different," Dylan said. "You're back now, though, and we've got this. Right now." She squeezed Frankie's hands gently.

She held her breath, hoping Frankie would say something about staying longer, about extending what they had. She thought about asking her outright to stay, but she was too afraid of the answer.

Frankie nodded. "You're right. The past is behind us, and we've got more important things to worry about. We've got one week left to make sure the Pumpkin Finale is bigger and better than it's ever been." Frankie's eyes were clear now, no trace of tears.

Dylan exhaled. That wasn't exactly the reply she was looking for, but Frankie was right. Saving the library took precedence. And Dylan couldn't blame Frankie for leaving again now that she knew the extent of the pain she had experienced here. "One week." She scrunched her eyes shut as if she had a migraine.

"We can do it," Frankie said, squeezing Dylan's hands now. "Let's save the library."

Those words seemed to pop the bubble of tension between them. Dylan let out a breath, and Frankie's shoulders relaxed.

"Let's save the library," Dylan repeated with as much conviction as she could muster.

Dear Library Board,

I teach English at Juniper Creek High School, and I spend much of my time in the Juniper Creek Library looking for books to discuss with my class and looking for teaching materials. This library has been integral to my teaching process since I started working at the school many years ago (longer than I care to admit).

My wife always loved the library as well. She used to go there weekly to check out a book or two, and I'd find her curled up on our couch with her nose buried in the pages.

We lived in Vancouver when our daughter was growing up, and we always took her to libraries there. Now we take my granddaughter to the Juniper Creek Library when she visits, and the joy on her face always makes me smile.

I appreciate the work you do on the board, and I know you understand the importance of libraries to everyone in this area. I hope you can help us raise funds to keep this library and the rest in the region open for the foreseeable future.

Thank you,
Julián Flores

CHAPTER TWENTY-FIVE

FRANKIE

Frankie was meeting Dylan at the library on Monday so they could finalize everything for the market. Dylan usually had Mondays off, but she was in the library that day to work on a few tasks for the Pumpkin Finale. With every day that passed, they inched closer to the last event and closer to either succeeding or failing with fundraising.

Despite the ticking clock, Frankie took her time that morning at the Bluebell. She brought her laptop with her down to breakfast and touched up her photos; she'd found a place in Abbotsford that would print them for her, and Evvie had offered to pick them up on Thursday when she went to her queer seniors' group. Frankie had ordered a couple canvases and lots of prints to sell at the market.

As she worked, she ran through her conversation with Dylan the day before. That had been the only time they'd explicitly talked about what had happened on the day Frankie left. On the day they'd each made a choice that had set the course for the rest of their lives. Frankie had often imagined how that conversation would go, and she thought she'd feel better after talking it through, but she didn't.

All it did was bring up all the *what ifs* that Frankie had run through time and time again. What if Frankie hadn't left? What if Frankie had waited and told Dylan her secret first? What if she'd waited to tell Ma and Wing Keung? What if she'd told Dylan *before* she got engaged?

Speculating was no use, and, as always, it made Frankie's heart ache.

All she could do now was take each day as it came. They were friends again, maybe more than friends. Even if it didn't last, it was better than nothing.

She opened her computer and checked her email. There was another email from her realtor in France. Audaciously, the movie company had raised their offer yet again and were still pushing to buy the cottage.

Frankie had saved up for years for that cottage. It was on the outskirts of a small town not unlike Juniper Creek, and the surrounding countryside was idyllic. It was the perfect location for both sweeping landscape shots and intimate personal portraits. Which was probably why the movie company wanted it.

Frowning, she went to click *delete* but hesitated. The cottage didn't mean *that* much to her, really. Maybe it was best to keep her options open.

There was another unexpected email in her inbox from one of her contacts at National Geographic. Her interest piqued, Frankie opened it and scanned the contents. They wanted her to come out of retirement to take on a project in India. Her instinct was to reply with an enthusiastic *yes!* But she hesitated. The project would start on November 2, so they'd need her to fly out on the 31st at the latest. She'd be going straight from Juniper Creek to India without any downtime at her cottage in between.

She hadn't booked her flight back to France yet, which made the scheduling easier, but she hadn't booked that flight for a reason. She didn't know if she was ready to leave Juniper Creek. After avoiding it for so many years, she thought she'd hate being here, but she enjoyed being at the Bluebell and participating in the Pumpkin Days events. And Dylan was here.

What if she said yes to the project and then Dylan asked her to stay?

She leaned back in her chair and looked around at the B&B's dining room. A father and his daughter sat at a table by the wall, eating breakfast and chatting quietly. Dean was in the kitchen, concocting something that smelled delicious. And the top of Olivia's head peeked up over the back of the antique couch where she sat reading, as usual.

Frankie closed her laptop without replying to the email and slid it into her satchel. She needed to talk to Dylan.

At the library, Dylan was shelving books and talking to the lady who had recommended *From the Ashes* to Frankie. Frankie didn't want to interrupt, so she made herself comfortable at one of the tables. She pulled her laptop out of her bag and plugged it in, but she didn't want to open it yet because her email would still be on the screen. Instead, she pulled out one of the romance books Olivia had loaned her and tried her best to immerse herself in the story.

"Hey," Dylan said, coming up to her a few minutes later. "Oh, that's a good one." She gestured to the book in Frankie's hands.

"Olivia said the same thing," Frankie said, smiling. She closed the book. "Are you ready to go over the vendor list?"

"Sure." Dylan pulled out the chair beside Frankie and settled into it.

As Frankie opened her laptop, she steeled herself. "I want to ask you something before we look over everything."

Dylan clasped her hands on the table in front of her. "Okay. Shoot."

Frankie told her about the National Geographic project, watching Dylan's face closely as she did so. Dylan raised one eyebrow slightly and nodded, but Frankie didn't know what to read from that. "They need my response right away so they can send me details and organize my flights—or find another photographer."

The silence before Dylan answered seemed to stretch an uncomfortably long time, and Frankie's heart felt as if it would beat out of her chest.

"That . . . that sounds like a good opportunity," Dylan said, running a hand through her hair.

"It does?"

"Doesn't it? I mean, that's up to you. Do you want to go to India? You seem to love photography still."

Dylan smiled as she spoke, and Frankie's heartbeat slowed. There was no sadness in Dylan's voice, no indication that she would be upset if Frankie left. Any hope Frankie had of Dylan asking her to stay was snuffed out.

"I would love to go to India," Frankie said honestly. But did she want that right now? It seemed like what she really wanted wasn't going to happen.

"Then say yes," Dylan said. "You don't want to regret saying no, right? It would be a last hurrah before you go back to France." There wasn't even a tremble in her voice.

Frankie cleared her throat. "Right. Okay. I'll say yes, then."

"Good. Congrats."

"Thank you." This didn't feel like something worthy of congratulations.

"Ready to go over the vendor list?"

"I suppose."

It was difficult to focus after that conversation. Frankie knew for sure now that she didn't have a future with Dylan. She had an email to answer and flights to book, and she needed to ask Wing Keung to help sell the house when she left.

She should have been thrilled about what lay ahead of her, but that excitement was nowhere to be found.

CHAPTER TWENTY-SIX

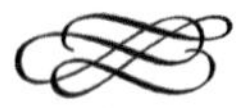

DYLAN

Dylan tried her best to keep her attention on the vendor spreadsheet. Frankie had just told her about the new project she was going to take on, which meant that she was definitely leaving Juniper Creek after the Pumpkin Finale. Dylan had known that was coming; if she hadn't been going to India, she would have been going back to France. But part of Dylan had hoped Frankie would stay this time. That she'd see how much Dylan still cared for her, and she'd stay.

Although Frankie hadn't exactly seemed excited about the new project proposal, she said she wanted to go to India. Dylan couldn't be selfish and tell her that she should say no just because Dylan didn't want her to go. She wouldn't hold Frankie back.

So Dylan did what she did best. She put everything Frankie had just told her into a mental box and shoved it as far back in her thoughts as she could. They needed to focus on the market now. The Pumpkin Finale was in less than a week, and they couldn't afford to spend mental energy on things they couldn't change.

Dylan pulled Frankie's laptop over so she could look at the spreadsheet in more detail. Frankie moved her chair slightly, so their knees were touching under the table. Part of Dylan wanted to pull away, but she made herself stay still. She got herself into this mess. She had agreed to help Frankie with Ma's house, and she had acknowledged that there was something between them. Something she had wanted to indulge in even though she knew it wouldn't last.

And she didn't want to keep pushing Frankie away, but if she kept getting closer, the pain of Frankie leaving would likely crush her.

"So, what do we have here?" Dylan asked, scanning the list of vendors. There were only two tables still open, which was good. Frankie had tallied up how much they'd make from vendor deposits, and although it wasn't enough to meet their goal, it was an impressive number. Dylan didn't think she could ask for much more than that.

Almost all the vendors from the Sunflower Festival were coming again—many of them local—and there were a few new ones that Dylan hadn't heard of. Those must have been the vendors Frankie found.

"Looks good," Dylan said. "I'm glad you remembered to book yourself a table."

"I wouldn't forget," Frankie said. "I even booked one for Margie. Gem pushed her to sell her paintings, and she finally gave in." She smiled, but it looked strained, like she wasn't quite happy about it. "Do we need to do anything else before we set up on Friday?"

"Nah. I need to do a few more things, but your part is done until then. Is there anything left to do on the house?"

She shook her head. "No. I've sold most of Ma's remaining furniture, so we'll have the money from that as well. As soon as Landon and Gerard are finished with repairs, we can get the house on the market. I'll probably be gone by then, though."

"Mm-hmm. Well, I'm glad most of it is done." Suddenly, Dylan couldn't sit there anymore. Reminders of Frankie leaving were everywhere, in everything they talked about. Her mental box wasn't staying where she had shoved it. "Let me know if I can help with anything else. I need to finish reshelving."

"Alright." Frankie closed her laptop. "Would you like to go for dinner? Dean told me about a nice place in downtown Abbotsford."

"Maybe. I might have too much to do, but I'll let you know." Dylan wanted to slap herself for not saying yes right away. Of course she wanted to go for dinner with Frankie. But the pain of losing her again was already tearing at her heart, eating at it like bookworms ate paper.

THEY ENDED up going out for dinner that night, and although Dylan held Frankie's hand and kissed her and shared another slice of chocolate cake with her, their dynamic wasn't the same. It was clear throughout their conversations that they were both avoiding the topic of Frankie leaving. They discussed the Pumpkin Finale, but that was as far as they'd go, as if the world would stop spinning once the festivities were over.

Dylan was so busy at the library for the rest of the week that she saw Frankie only in snatches of time here and there: a quick kiss on the cheek as Frankie mapped out the vendor tables, coffee at The June Bug on Tuesday for her afternoon break, a walk around the pond on Wednesday morning with the dogs.

Frankie took more photos on that walk, and Dylan snapped a photo of her own on her phone so she could save the image of Frankie in her element with Darcy and Bingley wagging their tails behind her. Frankie fit there, like she was meant to be in Juniper Creek, with Dylan and her dogs. A part of her family in a different way than she'd been before.

But that wasn't what Frankie wanted. She was going to fly off to India for one last hurrah as a National Geographic photographer, and then she'd settle down in France again. It was all too fucking easy to picture her taking photos of flowers outside her stone-walled cottage, ivy growing up the stones and lush countryside surrounding it, like something straight out of *The Secret*

Garden. She would be happy there, away from Ma's lingering presence in Juniper Creek. Away from Dylan.

Even though Evvie was at her queer group on Thursday night, Dylan turned down Frankie's invitation to dinner at the Bluebell. She needed time by herself before the Pumpkin Finale, before the entire town erupted in the chaos of preparing for the biggest day of fall. Even Halloween wouldn't be as festive—not after the events on Saturday.

And this Pumpkin Finale was more important than most. The fate of the library would be decided one way or another, and Dylan's fate would be decided with it.

Hello,

My name is Charlie, and I am a student at Juniper Creek High School. I'm also a writer, and I hope to publish my own books one day.

The library is one of my absolute favorite places to go. I spend a lot of time there with my best friend, and I love that I can check out books for free. If I had to pay to read as many books as I do, I would be broke in a heartbeat. And I probably wouldn't write as much as I do either.

Libraries are so important for bookish people but also for people who don't read much. So many things happen there like knitting groups, games nights, and workshops. Everyone goes there for one reason or another, and we can't take that away.

Please don't close our library!

Thank you,
Charlie Smith

CHAPTER TWENTY-SEVEN

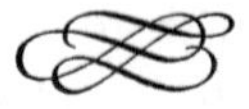

FRANKIE

Since Dylan declined her dinner invitation on Thursday, Frankie invited Margie instead. The two of them sat at the Bluebell eating carrot soup and apple brie paninis while Frankie told Margie about her job offer.

"I'm happy for you!" Margie said after a large bite of her sandwich. "But why don't *you* seem happy about it?"

Frankie's throat felt thick, so she took a sip of water. "I am excited. I haven't been to India yet, and I am itching to get behind a camera again in a professional sense. But . . . I don't know if I'm ready to leave."

Margie hummed in thought. "You do seem to fit in here, much more than you did when you were younger. And you and Dylan seem to be getting along well."

"We are. I think. I feel like we're just getting to know each other again." As she said the words, tears pushed up against the backs of her eyes.

"And if you leave, that won't continue?"

"No. I don't want a long-distance relationship." Not at her age.

"So then . . . why don't you stay? Or come back after your work in India?"

Frankie sighed. "I've been thinking about it. I haven't had a single romantic relationship that has turned out well, though. Something always happens, and I always end up leaving."

Margie pursed her lips. "When you say *something*, what do you mean?"

"I mean that we argue. Or I discover that our values don't align. Or we get into a situation that shows how we aren't suited for each other." Tension grew in Frankie's chest as she thought of all the things that could go wrong.

Nodding, Margie replied, "I can see why some of those things would cause you to leave, especially if you have the means to go. But isn't this different? You and Dylan were so close once upon a time. You probably know her better than you think you do because of that history, and even if the two of you argue, wouldn't you fight for her? Isn't there enough between you that you'd both work through it?"

Frankie's chest tightened more. "That's just it, though. What if I moved here and we decided to really be together, and then we couldn't work through whatever happened?"

"Well, you won't find out unless you try." Margie gave her a sad smile. "You have an opportunity here, and I wouldn't throw that away. You missed out on fifty years with her—do you really want to miss out on more? To keep wondering what could have happened?"

Margie had a point.

"I would give anything to have just one more hour with Henry," she continued. "But I can't. The chance is right here for you to have many more hours with Dylan."

Frankie nodded, blinking back tears. "You're right. I'll think about it."

After dinner, the two of them went to look at Ma's house, to see what it looked like after Landon and Gerard had been working on it. As far as Frankie could tell, the house looked ready to sell. Just in time for her to leave.

~

Frankie could sense something in the air on Friday—another storm, or simply a feeling of excitement? The Pumpkin Finale was the next day, and the entire town seemed to be in a state of anxious preparation. It wasn't even eight o'clock yet, and Olivia had been running up and down the stairs all morning, making sure the already-empty rooms were clean and ready for new guests. Dean was testing a new pumpkin pancake recipe, and he let Frankie try the first batch; it needed more cinnamon, but it was delicious.

She left him to his culinary devices and went across the street to The June Bug for a to-go cup of coffee. Jamie swept through the diner faster than usual, her hair a bit wild, a pencil behind each of her ears as if she'd forgotten she already had one there. "Hey," she said, practically skidding to a halt in front of where Frankie stood at the counter. "Here's your coffee. Going to set up for the market?" Frankie nodded. "Great! We are already so busy today—things are looking up for tomorrow!" With that, she grabbed a freshly brewed pot of coffee and wove between customers, refilling their mugs.

Frankie hoped Jamie was right.

She walked out to Main Street, looking down the road at all the shops. The sidewalks did seem more crowded than usual for this time of day, and there were a few shop owners out front adjusting their signage. The library wasn't open yet, so Frankie strolled down to peek into the shops. She'd been in all of them at least once now. Mabel's Antiques had a whole collection of vintage cameras, and it had been difficult for her to resist buying them all. She paused at the window and peered in at them.

"Good morning, Frankie," Eleanor said from one store down, bringing out a basket of dried flowers to place by the door of Thistles and Stems. "All ready for tomorrow?"

"I sure hope so," Frankie said.

Eleanor laughed. "Let me tell you, I underestimated the

Sunflower Festival in August. If the Pumpkin Finale is anything like it, you're in for a treat."

Waving goodbye to Eleanor, Frankie continued her stroll. Flora's Dairy Barn had a special on burnt caramel ice cream, which sounded good, but it was too early for a frozen treat, and it wasn't surprising that Flora's was one of the only slower shops. The bakery had a line out the front door already, and Cedar Logs art gallery was hosting a morning painting session. The sign out front said they would be painting a pumpkin patch.

Frankie crossed the street and walked back the other way toward the library. She peeked into Emily's Garden, but Minnie must have been in the back, so she moved on. Through the front windows of Yellow Brick Books, Frankie saw Leah shifting around the books on the fall display. Plastic jack-o'-lanterns flickered on top of a few stacks, and a cheesy cardboard vampire pointed to a display of paranormal reads.

Even Get Your Gear seemed to be in theme for the Finale. They were selling blow-up pumpkins, ghosts, and Frankenstein's monsters as well as pumpkins of all sizes. Dylan had mentioned that the blow-up ornaments would be on display at the park the following day along with a black-and-orange bouncy castle.

It was comforting to see the town coming together around a holiday. As she walked down the street, breathing in the cool fall air and sipping her coffee, she felt like she belonged. How could she leave this place when she was just getting to know it again? How could she leave Dylan?

When she got to the library, Hugo and Landon were unloading tables and chairs from a large delivery truck. "Oh, hey, Frankie," Landon said, waving at her before he hefted a folding table off the truck bed. "Dad is at your mom's place right now. We only have a couple of things left to do."

"Good morning, Landon." She raised her cup in his direction in greeting. "Not a problem. My brother is going to help with putting the house on the market, so there's no rush. I appreciate all the work you and your father have done, though. The place looks wonderful!"

"Excuse me," Hugo said, brushing past her with a stack of chairs. "This seems like a lot more tables and chairs than we had last year."

"That's because it is." Dylan stood just inside the sliding doors, her arms crossed and her stance wide as she supervised. She wore a dark purple plaid shirt today with her usual jeans and sneakers. The only spot of brightness on her outfit was her library name tag. "These are the tables for the park, plus the ones for the library. They wouldn't split the delivery for us."

"Of course." Hugo rolled his eyes.

"Good morning," Frankie said, leaning in to peck Dylan on the cheek. Dylan opened her arms and pulled Frankie in for a side hug.

"Welcome to the chaos," Dylan said, waving her arm out at the truck. "And this is only the tip of the iceberg." She kept her other arm around Frankie's waist, which was reassuring. Despite having turned down Frankie's offer for dinner, she seemed to be in a good mood.

Frankie finished off her coffee. "Jamie said the diner has been busy this morning, and the rest of Main Street looks busier than usual too."

Dylan turned her head so her nose touched Frankie's cheek. "I hope so," she said softly as the tip of her nose moved down Frankie's jawline, sending a shiver up Frankie's spine. "The last thing we need is a repeat of Saturday. We can't set up the tables until first thing in the morning tomorrow, but we can help with decorations. They've taken over the meeting room." She gestured inside.

"Okay. What can I do to help?"

As she had expected, she was put to work right away. Lorelai, Margie, and Gem were in the meeting room, which was an explosion of fall colors. "Evvie is better at this than I am. I wish she didn't have to work today," Gem grumbled as she tried to do . . .

something . . . with what looked to be a ball of orange tissue paper. "Oh, hi, Frankie."

"Good morning," Margie said, smiling at her.

"Frankie!" Lorelai swept over to her and gave her a quick hug. Frankie had only spoken to Lorelai a couple of times, but the mayor treated her like she was part of the town. "Thank you for coming to help. The pressure is on this year."

"I can see that." And she could feel it.

The four of them worked on decorations for the rest of the morning while Hugo and Landon finished unloading, and Dylan and Gwen managed library duties. They took a break for lunch at the diner. "Everything's on the house today," Jamie said, ignoring Lorelai's insistence that she would pay. "You're all working hard. You need the fuel."

In the afternoon, Iris came over to help, and a few more volunteers showed up too. Lorelai drew the layout of the festivities on the whiteboard in the meeting room, and they divvied up what needed to be done the next day so they could set up as quickly as possible. Instead of starting after lunch like the games day and the scavenger hunt had done, the Pumpkin Finale started at eleven and went until five. It was going to be a longer day, and they needed to use all that time to its greatest potential.

By four o'clock, Frankie was exhausted. She collapsed on one of the comfy chairs in the library's reading space. She hadn't even done a lot, really, but she knew how much the next day mattered. There wasn't much else they could do for the library at this point —almost all the funds were raised already, and they hadn't met their goal yet. Now they were relying on the entrance fees and any final donations.

Dylan plopped down into the chair next to her and laid her head back. "It's been a long day," she said, reaching over to grab Frankie's hand.

She had been busy today, but she'd stopped by the meeting room numerous times to kiss Frankie's cheek or rub her shoulders. Dylan sat next to Frankie at lunch, allowing Frankie to put her hand on her thigh. But even with all of that, she hadn't said anything about Frankie leaving in two days.

Frankie had considered bringing it up herself, but she didn't want to sway Dylan in one direction or the other. If Dylan wanted her to stay, she would say something. At least, Frankie hoped she would.

"You okay?" Dylan asked, squeezing her fingers.

"Yes, just tired. I can't imagine how busy tomorrow morning is going to be."

Dylan nodded. "It will be busy, but it will be worth it. It *has* to be." Her words echoed Evvie's from the previous Saturday.

"I think I'm going to go rest," Frankie said. She truly was tired, but she also hoped Dylan would show a sign that she wanted Frankie to stay. Would she ask Frankie to dinner? Or to come over for their last night before the Finale? After all, Frankie needed to pack and get a good night's sleep the next night because of her early flight on Sunday.

"Good idea," Dylan said, and Frankie's hopes fell. "I could use a nap before dinner. Are you coming in first thing in the morning?"

"Do you want me to?"

"Of course I do." Dylan's voice softened. "I want you to be with me for as long as you can be."

Frankie inhaled sharply. Did that mean Dylan wanted her to stay? Or did that mean she just wanted Frankie to be around all day the next day? It wasn't very clear, but it was the closest Dylan had come to saying she wanted Frankie around—and that's what Frankie needed to hear.

"Okay. I'll be here."

When she stood, Dylan stood with her and wrapped her arms around Frankie's shoulders. Frankie pushed her face into Dylan's neck, inhaling that faint lilac scent and trying not to cry. Dylan kissed her softly. It wasn't a long kiss, and it left her longing for more as she walked back to the Bluebell.

With only one full day left in Juniper Creek, she still didn't know exactly how Dylan felt about her. She acted like she wanted Frankie, but she had encouraged her to go to India and then back to France. Frankie shouldn't have let herself fall again, but she was in too deep now and there was nothing she could do.

She'd wait until the end of the next day to decide what she really wanted. Nothing was set in stone until she was on the plane.

CHAPTER TWENTY-EIGHT

DYLAN

When Frankie showed up at the library on Saturday morning wearing her black jacket and khakis, her camera bag hanging from her shoulder, Dylan was tempted to pull her into her office and stay in there for the day, just the two of them. They could spend the day together and forget about everything happening outside.

But that was wishful thinking. They barely had time for a quick kiss before they jumped into action. They needed to set up the market in the parking lot and across the street at the park before the Finale started at eleven, and everything needed to be perfect. This was their last chance to save the library.

Gwen oversaw the library that day, and they canceled all programming so she could more easily manage by herself. They had considered closing the library instead, but Dylan couldn't stand the thought of closing it if even one person still needed it.

"I'm here, I'm here!" Evvie cried, bursting through the library's sliding doors at half past nine. She was huffing and puffing, and she bent over with her hands on her knees for a moment. "Sorry, I had to open the clinic, or I would have been here sooner."

"It's okay. Thanks, Ev." Dylan pulled her friend close and gave her a squeeze. Evvie really needed a break from her job, but now was not the time to talk about it.

The tables and chairs had already been set up. Dylan directed everyone while Frankie helped the vendors, and Evvie helped wherever she was needed. Many of the vendors wanted to stop and chat, and Dylan had to rein in her instinct to tell them to shut up so she could keep working; she couldn't afford to get people on her bad side when their support was essential.

Minnie and Eleanor were there; each of them had booked a table, but they had pushed their tables together and placed their goods across the span of both. Daphne, Charlie's older sister, helped Minnie set up an array of flowers that could handle the colder October air while Eleanor set up stacks of her nonfiction book, *The Symbology of Flowers*. Dylan couldn't help the lump that formed in her throat at how well the two of them meshed—she wished she could be like that with Frankie.

Even though Frankie hadn't said anything about it lately, her leaving weighed heavily on Dylan's shoulders. This was the last full day she could spend with Frankie before she flew out to India, and she was painfully aware of that in every single second. It took all her energy to focus on the tasks in front of her, but she couldn't afford to let herself be distracted.

She couldn't stop Frankie from leaving, anyway, and she wasn't going to try. She wasn't going to put her desires before Frankie's. The flight was booked, and Frankie was leaving. That was that.

This—the Pumpkin Finale—was happening right here, and right now.

"Where shall I set up?" Elouise Mitchell asked, coming up to Dylan with a large wicker basket full of knitted animals. She was late, but Dylan wasn't about to nitpick.

"We've got a table ready for you," Dylan said, leading her over to Frankie. She was standing at her own table, her photographs set up on stands around her. Dylan recognized many of them from their trip to the wetlands. "Where is Elouise's table?"

Frankie squinted at the map she'd drawn up. "Oh, you're on the other side of the street," she said. "I'll show you. Dylan, will you please keep an eye on my table?"

Dylan nodded and watched the two of them go, smiling fondly after Frankie. Then she remembered that she wouldn't get to see Frankie around town much longer, and her throat thickened. She cleared it and turned to help Zoey set up her candle table, keeping an eye on Frankie's table as she did so.

"I come bearing fuel," Jamie said, striding over from the diner with a large carafe and a stack of paper cups. "Apple cider to keep everyone warm this morning. Want some?" She held out the stack to Dylan.

Dylan shook her head. "Unless it's spiked, I'll pass."

Jamie shrugged and headed for the table at the farthest end of the parking lot where a man was selling art made from secondhand books. It seemed fitting to put that vendor close to the library.

The rest of the morning went by in a blur, and before Dylan knew it, Lorelai was giving her opening speech from the gazebo. Dylan couldn't hear the words clearly from where she stood, but she didn't need to. She knew almost exactly what Lorelai would be saying anyway.

Evvie came over to her and half collapsed against her arm. "Here we go," she said. "Not much we can do now except cross our fingers and pray to Judy Garland."

Dylan grunted in response. Standing idle was not going to help her state of mind. "Want to walk around with me? I can't just stand here."

Evvie straightened her scarf. "Why don't you walk around with Frankie? I'll take over market duties for a bit. Everyone is set up already, so it's not a problem."

"She's got her table to run."

Evvie scoffed. "Come here." She dragged Dylan to Frankie's table. "Do you think I could run your table for a bit?" Evvie asked. "I'll give people your card if they have questions."

Frankie raised her eyebrows. "Sure . . . May I ask why?"

Evvie elbowed Dylan in the ribs.

"Oh, um. Would you like to walk around the festival with me?" Even after she had spent a large portion of the past three weeks with Frankie, nerves tickled Dylan's stomach as she asked that question, like she was a schoolgirl on her first date.

Or her last date, more accurately.

The smile that spread across Frankie's face lit up the whole world. "I'd love to. Let me grab extra business cards in case Evvie needs them. Thank you for covering for me, Evvie."

As Frankie ran inside, Dylan stood on the sidewalk and looked out over the festivities. Crowds had built over at the park, and a few people filtered across the street, browsing the tables in the parking lot. Laughter rang in the air, and children in costumes chased each other on the grass.

"I'm ready," Frankie said, coming up beside Dylan. She grabbed Dylan's hand firmly, and they headed across the street together.

They stopped at one of the two admission tables at the park entrance. "You don't have to pay admission, you know," Kat said when Dylan pulled out her wallet. "You're both volunteers."

"I know, but I want to." She handed over a twenty-dollar bill. Anything to help the library.

She relinked hands with Frankie, and her spirits lifted as they strolled through the park. The market on this side of the street was busy. There were all types of goods for sale: nonalcoholic beer, beard oil, fudge, baked goods, kitchen utensils, and chocolate.

They stopped by Margie's table to say hello to her and Gem, and Frankie bought one of her paintings. "We'll figure out the shipping later," she said, then they continued on.

"These are so cute!" Frankie said as they came upon a vendor selling coats for dogs. "You have to get one for Darcy and Bingley." She picked up a red plaid dog jacket. "This one, so they can match you!"

Dylan laughed, tension easing out of her shoulders. "Okay. What about for the other one?"

"Do you have another color for the plaid?" Frankie asked the vendor, a stout woman wearing a brown leather jacket.

"I do," she said. "I've got blue, yellow, or purple."

"Let's do . . . the yellow." Frankie held the jackets while Dylan paid. "These would be perfect for that photoshoot I mentioned!"

Dylan opened her mouth to reply, but the words caught in her throat. There would be no photoshoot because Frankie was leaving. There was a beat of silence before Frankie asked the vendor for a bag, then the two of them continued to walk around, not saying anything.

The speaker nearest them crackled slightly as Lorelai's voice said, "The costume contest is starting soon! If you've entered already, please come line up at the gazebo. If you haven't entered yet, you have ten minutes left to do so."

A trio of kids dressed as a vampire, a werewolf, and a witch ran in front of them, giggling. A moment later, Ben followed, wearing a large round rocky-looking thing with colored pipe cleaners in a ring around it.

He spotted Dylan and stopped in front of them. "Like my costume?" he said, holding his arms out to the sides, although he couldn't really do much else with them.

"Um, yeah," Dylan replied. "What are you, exactly?"

Ben scoffed. "Saturn, obviously."

"Of course," Frankie said, elbowing Dylan lightly. "We knew that. You look *just* like Saturn."

A smile brightened Ben's face. "Thanks. I'm gonna win the contest." With that, he continued toward the gazebo with his head held high.

"I hope he wins," Frankie said, grinning at Dylan. "It probably took his mom ages to get those pipe cleaners to sit that way."

A line of tables was set up at the far end of the park, each of them covered in black garbage bags. One large pumpkin sat on each table, along with an assortment of carving tools in buckets.

Behind each table was a different person, clearly waiting for a cue to start carving.

Frankie pulled Dylan over to Gerard, who sat behind one of the tables. "Hello," Frankie said. "Do I have time to thank you for your work on my mother's house?"

Gerard shrugged. "It was nothing, really."

"Well thank you, anyway. Are you carving a pumpkin?"

He smoothed his large mustache down over his lips and eyed his pumpkin. "I am. I enter the contest every year."

Dylan scoffed. "You're being modest," she said to Gerard. Turning to Frankie, she said, "He fucking *wins* the pumpkin-carving contest every year."

Frankie's eyes widened. "Oh! Should I congratulate you early, then? Or should I say, 'good luck'?"

"I don't want to count my chickens," he said.

"Well, good luck then."

They moved on, stopping at a candy kiosk so Frankie could buy a small bag of candy corn.

"I can't believe you like that stuff," Dylan said, wrinkling her nose. "It's disgusting."

Frankie popped a piece in her mouth. "It's delicious."

Dylan rolled her eyes. "Let me show you something that's actually good." She led Frankie over to a temporary structure that had been set up by the baseball diamond. The walls were painted black, the front door was covered with a tattered black cloth, and mist from dry ice rolled around their feet. Spooky noises echoed from the inside, along with a few good-natured screams.

Iris stood out front in a gimmicky wedding dress, fake blood painted in a line across her neck and her face painted an eerie white. "Welcome to the haunted house," she said, drawing out her words. "Do you dare go inside?"

Frankie looked at Dylan and made an *oooo* noise. She put her bag of candy corn in her pocket. "It's not quite as scary in the daytime, though, is it?"

Dylan shrugged. "It's still fun."

The two of them walked up to the entrance, and Iris wiggled her fingers at them in farewell. Frankie pushed Dylan in first, and the light from outside dimmed as they made their way into the haunted house.

Dylan usually went through with Evvie, but it was nice to have Frankie clinging to her arm.

"Is it just me, or is it colder in here?" Frankie asked.

Dylan didn't reply but pulled her forward. As they rounded a corner, a black shape swooped at them from the ceiling. Frankie shrieked in Dylan's ear, and Dylan laughed. This was more fun than she had anticipated. They continued on, running into a skeleton on the wall, a mummy climbing out of a sarcophagus, and a ghost that chased them out the door on the other side of the house.

Frankie shivered and shook out her hair. "I swear there were spiders in there," she said, laughing breathlessly. "I thought Hijiri was helping with the house too."

"Who do you think the ghost was?" Dylan smirked.

Frankie swatted her arm playfully. "Is there anything else to see? I should be getting back to my table."

"We can go back. You've seen all the important things."

As the two of them walked back, Dylan realized she had managed to forget that Frankie was leaving, if only for a few minutes.

CHAPTER TWENTY-NINE

FRANKIE

The festival stayed busy right until five o'clock. Frankie had seen Dylan a few more times throughout the day, and she was looking happier. They had favorable chances of hitting their goal. At least, Frankie thought so, and her affirmation for the day was *We will succeed*. Nobody would know the actual numbers until later that evening.

Although Frankie felt exhausted right down to her bones, and everyone else probably did too, she helped the other vendors clear away their things and waited in the library with Dylan, Evvie, Minnie, and Eleanor until Lorelai, Iris, and Hijiri came in with the tills and debit machines. It was time to tally the numbers.

The core team of the Friends of the Library was there, gathered around in the meeting room, anxiously awaiting the verdict. The tension in the air was so thick it seemed to slow everyone's movements.

"I can't work with everyone hovering over me," Iris said as she began counting the first till. The red on her neck had rubbed off on the top of her dress, making her look even more ghastly. They all gave her space, attempting to make conversation in the library foyer until she called them in.

Iris's face didn't give anything away, and she was even harder to read behind all that white face paint. Frankie held Dylan's hand and could feel her practically vibrating. No one cared about the library more than Dylan. Frankie loved that about her, but it also made her nervous.

Whatever Iris announced could crush Dylan.

"Well?" Dylan asked, bouncing on her toes. Her grip on Frankie's hand became progressively tighter, and Frankie wouldn't be able to feel her fingers soon.

Iris's lower lip trembled, and that's when Frankie knew. Iris shook her head, but Frankie didn't hear the number she announced because she was paying too much attention to Dylan, who had let go of Frankie and stood scarily still.

They hadn't done it.

They hadn't raised enough to save the library.

Evvie reached for Dylan, and that's when Frankie knew things were worse than she'd expected.

Without a word, Dylan turned and fled to her office.

"I'll go talk to her," Frankie said to Evvie, who nodded and wrung her hands.

When Frankie knocked on the door, there was no response. She turned the doorknob and stuck her head in. "Can I come in?"

Dylan didn't answer and instead paced to her desk, flexing her hands open and closed while breathing heavily.

Frankie gently grabbed her shoulders, turning her around and pulling her close, but Dylan was stiff as a board against Frankie's chest.

"It's okay," Frankie said. "We will get through this."

That sentence seemed to knock life back into Dylan, who shook her head and blinked rapidly.

"*We* will get through this?" she said, pushing Frankie away. "You don't have to deal with this at all. You're going to India tomorrow morning. I'll be stuck here, with *nothing*." She gasped and staggered as if she struggled to stay upright. "I don't know how this happened. I don't . . . I should have done more. I should have gone door-to-door, or written letters to people, or *something*.

If I had got that ad in on time, we could have made enough. But I let myself get distracted, and I spent too much time with you . . ."

Those words were like an arrow through Frankie's chest. *I spent too much time with you . . .*

Dylan ran her hands through her hair and fell into her desk chair. Frankie felt her face hardening, her shell going up.

When Dylan finally looked at her and saw her expression, she bolted up from her chair. "Shit, Frankie, that's not what I meant. I—"

Frankie held up a hand. She didn't want to hear anymore.

She heard what Dylan meant. Dylan had spent too much time with her, and that meant she hadn't spent enough time on the library. It wasn't logical to blame the failure of the library on Frankie, but of course Dylan would pull that out as an excuse. Clearly, Frankie wasn't as important to Dylan as Dylan was to Frankie.

This was Dylan's engagement all over again.

"You know what," Frankie said, looking at Dylan's shoes rather than at her face. "I hoped that everything could work out between us this time. This was our chance to be together in a different world. But you can never see past the front of your nose, can you? You're so single-minded. I've always loved how much you love the things you're passionate about, but you shut out everything else, and it's not healthy. Juniper Creek may have changed, but you haven't."

She raised her gaze to Dylan's face. Dylan's mouth was open slightly, her brows drawn together.

Frankie continued, "You said I had a point when I brought up how work was your whole life, but I don't think you actually absorbed what I meant." She looked up at the ceiling, trying to keep her tears from overflowing. "I'm glad I'm leaving." Her voice broke. "If I stayed, you would always choose someone or something else. Just like last time."

Before Dylan could respond, Frankie spun on her heel and left, slamming the door behind her.

CHAPTER THIRTY

DYLAN

Dylan wasn't about to let Frankie go that easily, not after a comment like that. Pushing out of her chair, she ran after her and caught up to her in the library foyer. She grabbed Frankie's arm, and Frankie whipped around to face her, her brown eyes blazing.

"Don't you dare tell me that I chose someone else," Dylan said, trying to keep her voice down. Everyone else was in the meeting room, and they didn't need to hear this. "You were always first in my life, Frankie, always! How was I supposed to know that you were in love with me? I didn't even know that was an option back then. I got married because I thought I was in love, and I thought that's what I was supposed to do. You're the one who left! What your mother said to you was awful, but don't you *dare* blame your decision to leave on me."

She was shocked at herself for saying that, but she had believed that Frankie's absence had been her fault for years, and now—after spending more time with Frankie and getting the full story—she knew that it wasn't. Sure, she'd played a role in Frankie's decision to leave, but it had been *Frankie's decision*.

Tears welled up in Frankie's eyes and spilled over as she took a step closer to Dylan. When she spoke, her voice was quiet but unsteady. "I just wanted you to pick me. No one ever chose me, Dylan. My dad left us, I was never good enough for Ma, and this town was a gilded cage. Your life was perfect. You were happy, and you were going to marry your high school sweetheart! I was stuck on the sidelines, watching you, wanting to be where *he* was. Wanting to be myself. But I could never be. Not back then. And you didn't see that."

Dylan shook her head. "You didn't even ask me for help, Frankie. You didn't even tell me *why* you were leaving. You pushed me away, not the other way around. It was *your* fault our relationship ended that day. You didn't give me a choice."

Her voice was definitely louder now, but she wasn't in control of her emotions enough to lower it. She glared at Frankie.

Frankie glared back. "Well, what about now? Who's doing the pushing now?"

"You are! You're leaving. You can't fault me for being upset about losing the thing I dedicated my life to. Unlike you, we can't all just leave when we're upset."

CHAPTER THIRTY-ONE

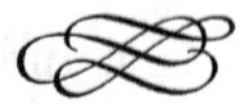

FRANKIE

Frankie rocked back on her heels as if Dylan's words were a solid projectile. They sure felt like one, smacking her in the chest with enough force to take her breath away.

Dylan's eyes were more than stormy now. The blue of her irises was a vortex that threatened to pull Frankie in and drown her.

Without another word, Frankie turned and marched out of the library.

She went straight to her room at the Bluebell, not even greeting Olivia, who was flipping through a stack of papers at the front desk.

Frankie collapsed on her bed and stared at the ceiling. She hadn't even bothered to turn on the light. A ball of tension sat in her chest and she wanted to sob it out, but her tears seemed to have dried up. It's not that she believed what Dylan said; she didn't, not by a long shot.

She hadn't been pushing Dylan away, and she didn't "run away" just because she was upset.

She left because she needed to. Because staying meant she

would get hurt. "My needs and wants are important," she whispered to herself.

Dylan had built the strongest wall between them that she'd ever put up, and there was no way Frankie was getting over it or through it. She didn't even want to anymore. That wall could stay where it was for all she cared.

She made herself get off the bed and turn on the light, and she grabbed her laptop on the way back. Propping herself up against the headboard, she opened her laptop and the email with her flight details. She could have checked in to her flight that morning, but she hadn't, just in case. Now, there was no reason for her not to.

She filled in her details, picked her seat, and double checked it all. But she couldn't bring herself to click the last "check-in" button. She growled in frustration and got up to pack.

It took only ten minutes for her to gather all her things. Then she grabbed her laptop again and hovered over the "check-in" button.

There was nothing holding her back. Not only had she lost the library, she had also lost Dylan.

CHAPTER THIRTY-TWO

DYLAN

After Frankie stormed out, Dylan felt multiple sets of eyes on her and turned to see everyone in the meeting room staring in her direction. As soon as she looked at them, most of them turned away. But Evvie didn't.

Her best friend walked over and stopped a good foot in front of her, knowing that Dylan liked her space when she was going through something. "Are you okay?" she asked.

Dylan shook her head and didn't stop Evvie as she wrapped her arms around her.

"I'm sorry," Evvie said. "That didn't sound great."

"It wasn't," Dylan whispered. She couldn't bring herself to speak louder than that. Everything felt too loud in that moment, too much. How could anything be normal right now? "I need to go home." She cleared her throat.

"Do you want me to come with you?"

Dylan shook her head again.

"Okay. You know you can call me if you need me."

The walk home seemed to pass in no time at all. Before Dylan knew it, she was standing in her kitchen feeding Darcy and Bingley their dinner. Her hands were numb, and she felt as if she was floating over herself, watching her body go through her normal evening tasks. She didn't have the energy to make dinner, so she poured herself a bowl of cereal. She wasn't hungry, but it felt good to be doing something.

Sitting down on the couch, she turned the TV on. A streaming service was still on the screen, displaying the cover for the 2005 version of *Pride and Prejudice*. Dylan clicked play and tried to lose herself in the film, but she couldn't absorb what was happening. She'd seen the movie a million times, but it wasn't making sense.

She must have fallen asleep at some point because she woke up with the light of the TV on her face, the movie over. Darcy and Bingley snored on the floor in front of her. Sighing, she got up slowly and made her way to bed.

It was eight o'clock when she woke again. Sunlight peeked in through her bedroom window, and a bird sang somewhere nearby. Dylan rubbed her eyes, which were swollen and dry. As soon as she moved, Bingley lifted her head from the bottom of the bed to look at Dylan, and Darcy huffed at her.

"Okay, okay," Dylan said, stretching. "I'm getting up."

As she went through her morning routine—brushing her teeth, combing her hair, washing her face, making herself coffee—the events of the day before flooded her mind. She held the news of the library's closure at a distance. They would close one day soon, but until then, she would go about her life as usual. There wasn't anything else she could do.

The fight she had with Frankie was more present in her memory, the pain more acute. She had meant most of what she'd said, but that wasn't the time and place to air those things. And her last comment about Frankie leaving . . . that had been aimed to wound.

She'd been upset about the library closing and angry at Frankie for saying she was single-minded. Dylan cared about a lot of things; in fact, she cared so much that it overwhelmed her at times. But she understood her priorities.

Yes, she had struggled to balance preparing for Pumpkin Days with spending time with Frankie, but that didn't mean she was single-minded. Many people struggled with balance. Didn't they?

She ran the last few weeks through her mind. It was true that she could have been more open with Frankie about her feelings. She hadn't been completely vulnerable because she was scared about what that would do to her. Every time she did something for herself or was honest about what she wanted, someone else got hurt: when she'd told Frankie she was engaged, she'd unknowingly crushed her; when she told her husband she was gay, she had ruined their relationship and broken his trust in her.

But not telling Frankie how she felt had ruined things this time. Then it hit her: She had started working at the library because of Frankie. The library was an essential link between them. And in trying to save that link, she'd pushed away the reason it mattered in the first place.

She groaned and ran her hands through her hair. Maybe if she had asked Frankie to stay—if she had been honest about what she wanted—she wouldn't be in this position.

She put on Darcy's and Bingley's harnesses and pulled on her vest. If she gave in to the urge to wallow, she'd be stuck inside until Evvie came to drag her out. She needed to get moving.

As she stepped outside, she inhaled the crisp fall air. It reminded her of being at the wetlands with Frankie, watching her snap photos. She'd had that smile on her face, the warmth in her voice that showed how much she truly loved photography.

Darcy and Bingley pulled Dylan along toward the pond, which was their favorite place to walk. When they got to the end of the street, Dylan halted in her tracks and looked toward the Bluebell.

Frankie's flight had been at six. She would be long gone by now, and she wasn't coming back.

CHAPTER THIRTY-THREE

FRANKIE

Frankie had missed her flight. She hadn't left the Bluebell yet, or her room for that matter. Every time she went to open the door, something stopped her. She thought about booking another flight, but the trip wasn't exciting to her anymore.

She emailed her contact at National Geographic and apologized, saying that something urgent had come up and she couldn't be part of the project. She wasn't lying, exactly. Something urgent *had* come up; she'd urgently changed what she wanted. It wasn't like National Geographic could fire her, but she didn't want to leave them in the lurch, so she emailed a few of her photographer friends and referred them for the project.

Then she called Wing Keung. "Of course you can stay with us," he said. "We'd love to have you. Sit tight, and I'll come pick you up."

She brought her bags down to the foyer and put them against the wall, then she went to the dining area. "Good morning," Dean said. "Weren't you supposed to be gone earlier?"

"Yes," Frankie replied. "I decided to visit with my brother in Vancouver for a bit instead."

"That sounds nice. Can I get you anything for breakfast?"

She ordered the spicy omelet and picked up a romance book Olivia had left on the sideboard, attempting to read it while she ate. Her efforts were fruitless, and she was relieved when Olivia came to join her. The two of them talked about the book until Wing Keung phoned her to let her know he was out front.

"Thank you for everything," Frankie said. "You were both fantastic hosts." She hugged both Olivia and Dean.

"You're always welcome here," Olivia said, her smile warm. "Don't be a stranger."

Frankie cracked the window as soon as she got into Wing Keung's car. Neither of them said anything until they got onto the highway.

"So, why the change of heart?" he asked.

She licked her lips, wondering how to answer that question. She'd been thinking about it all morning. "I don't want to go back to work. I can still shape stories through leisure photography, and there's less pressure that way."

"Okay." He glanced at her. "But what about France?"

This part was tougher. "I like my cottage. It took me a while to save up for it, and I thought I would spend the rest of my life there." She watched the trees fly by out the window.

"But . . . ?"

"But I don't have family there. I'd be a long flight away from you, and I want to spend more time here. I don't . . . I don't want to leave again."

Wing Keung jolted his head back in surprise. "You don't want to leave . . . at all?"

"At all. I want to stay."

Wing Keung's jaw dropped. "Who are you, and what have you done with my sister?"

Frankie shrugged, trying not to cry.

They drove for another few minutes in silence. She got the feeling that Wing Keung was digesting her news. She was still digesting it herself.

"So, what are you going to do about your cottage?"

She'd thought through this part already. It hadn't been an easy decision, but she could admit now that she'd never felt like the cottage would be home. "A movie company wants to buy it, probably to use as a set. I brushed off their offer earlier, but I'm going to take it."

"Really?"

"Yes. And I'm going to donate the proceeds to the library." Her voice steadied as she spoke her plan out loud.

"Wow, okay." He rubbed his jaw. "If you're selling your cottage and you're living here, where are you going to live? Are you moving back to Juniper Creek?"

Frankie laughed wryly as a jolt of pain shot through her chest. "Definitely not. Would you mind if I stay with you until I figure it out?"

Wing Keung frowned. "I don't mind, but . . . Are you sure you've thought about this enough? This is what you really want?"

She nodded.

Her brother went to say something, but he stopped and puffed out his cheeks. He kept glancing at her, his forehead wrinkled.

"Out with it," she said. "What do you want to ask?"

"Well . . . What about Dylan?"

She had been expecting this question too, but it hurt nonetheless. "What about her? She's got her life, and I've got mine."

No matter how much she wanted to be with Dylan, Dylan had made it clear yesterday that she didn't understand Frankie at all.

But Frankie had found a way to save the library, and she was going to do it—for herself, and for everyone who benefited from library services. She could live here, close to the town where she grew up and the woman she had loved, and be happy knowing she had made a difference in people's lives with this decision. She would save the library that had once saved her.

That would have to be enough.

CHAPTER THIRTY-FOUR

DYLAN

Even though Dylan didn't usually work on Mondays, she went into the library. There wouldn't be any more days off for her.

A shadow of foreboding followed her everywhere she went, but it seemed oddly detached from her work. It was strange to keep the library running when it would be closing in a few weeks, but she knew it mattered to so many people. And, of course, she would do her best to make the library's last days mean something.

But the foreboding came from somewhere else. Somewhere under her ribs. It seemed to surface every time she caught herself wondering where Frankie was and how she was doing. Was she as devastated about the library as Dylan was? Would she forgive Dylan for what she had said? What if history repeated itself and they never spoke to each other again?

The day went by both too slowly and too quickly for Dylan's liking. Too slowly because Dylan couldn't stop thinking about Frankie, and too quickly because each minute that passed brought the library closer to closing.

Evvie came over to her house that evening for dinner. She said she just wanted something to do, but Dylan suspected it was to comfort her more than anything.

"How are you doing?" Evvie asked.

Dylan shook her head as she put a pizza in the oven. "I haven't keeled over yet." She sat down at the kitchen table beside her best friend. "You?"

"I'm alright. Work is . . . not fun. I mean, I love the animals and our clients, but I'm exhausted."

"I bet."

The two of them sat in silence for a moment, and when Dylan didn't say anything else, Evvie's forehead wrinkles creased further as she looked at Dylan with concern. "I'm sorry we didn't raise enough money."

Waving a hand, Dylan said, "It's fine. Well, it's not fine, but . . . This might sound strange. I need you to tell me if it doesn't make sense."

Evvie nodded. "Go on."

Dylan took a deep breath. "I . . . I keep thinking about Frankie."

Evvie's eyes softened.

"I meant most of what I said to her, but I shouldn't have said it that way. And since then . . . since she left, I . . ." Her throat closed around the words.

"You miss her?" Evvie put her hand on Dylan's arm.

The steadiness of Evvie's hand gave Dylan the push she needed to keep talking. "I do. More than I thought I would. When I found out we didn't raise enough for the library, of course I was devastated. But I think that was the book that broke the bookshelf—losing the library and losing Frankie had become one and the same." She took a shaky breath. "I had been trying so hard to tell myself that I was okay with Frankie leaving, that we could be together for a couple weeks and then I could move on. But . . . I don't want to move on, Evvie. Is that strange? Did I push Frankie away again? Did I do this to myself?"

Her best friend squeezed her arm gently. "It's not strange. You love her, and strong emotions like that often explode out of us when we least expect them and in ways we can't anticipate. But you didn't push her away. She could have stayed, if she wanted."

Dylan sighed, knowing that Evvie was right but not feeling any better about it. "You would think that by our age, I would have learned to hold on to the things that actually matter. But apparently, I still can't tell what those things are until it's too fucking late."

"If it's meant to be, it'll still happen," Evvie said, scooching closer to Dylan and wrapping her arms around Dylan's shoulders.

Dylan leaned her head against Evvie's. "Thanks, Ev." She didn't buy into the idea of anything as "meant to be," but she was grateful for Evvie's optimism.

~

AT WORK ON TUESDAY, Dylan did her best to be present. To notice the things around her that she took for granted. She was mourning the library, but at the same time she had accepted that her life was changing. If only she had accepted that before Frankie left.

She thought of calling her daughters that evening, of seeing what their schedules were so she could visit. She hadn't traveled much, and now she'd have more than enough time for it.

Before she got off shift, she picked up one of the bird books Frankie had been using. Birding seemed like a nice, quiet hobby to get into now that she'd have more time, but birds reminded her of Frankie. Especially cranes. She sighed and put the book down again.

Dylan suspected she'd feel a bit lost without work, but retiring didn't have to be all bad if she put in some effort. If she did something for herself, something she hadn't had the time or energy for before. Being with Frankie had reminded her that there was more to life than one's career, and she saw that in Evvie's situation as well.

On Wednesday, she spent the morning cleaning toys and

answering emails. Many patrons had messaged her, concerned about where they could go for resources and what would happen to the books they currently had on hold. She found herself explaining the same things so many times that she typed up a few canned emails to save herself the effort.

A knock on her office door drew her attention away from her current email.

It was Samaira, which was odd. Although she was the library manager, Samaira rarely came into the library in person, and when she did, she let Dylan know she was coming. She wore an orange dress and a smart-looking pair of black pumps. Her long wavy brown hair was pulled up in a loose bun. “Long time, no see,” Dylan said, standing to give her a hug.

When they parted, Samaira was smiling. “I should have come in sooner. I wanted to make the Pumpkin Finale at least, but my daughter had a ballet recital that I couldn’t miss. How are you?”

Dylan ran a hand through her hair. “Oh, you know. Surviving.” Her heart pounded. Was Samaira here to tell her that the library was closing sooner than she thought? But if that was why she had come, why was she smiling? “You?”

“I’m really good, actually. I’ve got news for you, and I wanted to share it in person.”

“Oh?”

“Let’s go get the others, too.”

Dylan scrunched her brow in confusion. Her news must concern the library if she wanted to tell Hugo and Gwen at the same time. They had also decided to work every day until the library closed. Who needed days off when you wouldn’t even have a job soon?

Samaira pulled the three of them into the meeting room. Hugo tilted his head at Dylan, and she shrugged. Gwen just stood there with wide eyes, her hands clasped demurely in front of her.

“This month has been a wild ride,” Samaira said.

Hugo barked out a laugh. “You can say that again.”

She nodded. “I’ve got news that isn’t any less wild, but I have a feeling it will make you all feel better. Yesterday evening, the board got a phone call that changed everything. There has been an anonymous donation of over five hundred thousand dollars to the library board."

Dylan's jaw dropped.

"It's enough to renovate our buildings and expand our collection. More than that, it's enough to keep all five libraries open." When everyone stayed frozen, she added, "Including the Juniper Creek Library."

Gwen fell back into a chair, her hand on her chest, and Hugo whooped and launched himself at Dylan. They both just about fell over backward, but he managed to keep them upright.

"How . . . sorry, what?" Dylan pinched herself to make sure she wasn't dreaming. Where had all that money come from? A grin grew on her face, and suddenly she was laughing. She grabbed Hugo's hands, and the two of them jumped around in a circle as if they were kids again.

Samaira laughed with them. "Congratulations," she said. "The library is staying open!"

Dear Library Board,

When I was eleven, my family moved to Juniper Creek. I never truly belonged with my mother and my brother, and my father had left us. I didn't belong in Juniper Creek either, but the one place I did belong was the library.

At the library, I was encouraged to be myself, to learn and explore and be messy. A librarian showed me how to use a camera, and I fell in love with photography there. I picked up as many books as I could about the art of photography, and I'd spend hours flipping through coffee table books just to look at the pictures. When I bought my own camera, I would get the pictures developed and look through them between the stacks. Photography became my passion and my career.

More importantly than that, I met my best friend and the love of my life at the library. We were in different grades at school, but we'd study together and read books with each other. We joined the summer reading programs and participated in library activities whenever we could because they were free and accessible, and they gave us a safe space to be together away from our families. We learned about life together, and the library was always our meeting place.

I came back to town later in life because my mother passed away, and when I found out the library was in trouble, I knew I needed to do whatever I could to help it. Libraries are some of the most vital places on this planet, and I've traveled the world, so that's saying a lot. I know that this library won't close because the world won't let it. It has too much value, and I hope you can see that.

From,
Frankie Chan

CHAPTER THIRTY-FIVE

FRANKIE

Frankie sat on Wing Keung's sofa, watching a show about flipping houses. It wasn't holding her attention, but she had nothing else to do. She needed to buy a car so she could drive herself around, but she'd have to wait until Ma's house sold to do that. She only had her savings left now that she'd donated all the money from the cottage to the library board.

How had Dylan taken the news? Frankie imagined it had gone over well. She wished she could have been there to see the expression on Dylan's face when she found out the library wasn't closing, but that wasn't her place anymore.

That thought made Frankie restless, and she got up to go for a walk. Wing Keung lived in a large neighborhood with a walking path around the outside, so it was easy for her to get in her daily exercise. She brought her camera along just in case.

As she walked, she ran through the argument she'd had with Dylan. She'd gone through it over and over again since she'd left Juniper Creek, and every time, she felt a nudge to go back to town. What Dylan said had hurt, but she hadn't been entirely wrong.

The more Frankie thought about it, the more she felt sure that this time, she had fled. And maybe last time she had been fleeing too. She didn't know how to work through conflict on this level, so instead of staying to face it head on, she ran away.

Maybe if she had stayed fifty years ago, she could have at least been friends with Dylan, and maybe it would have evolved into something else later in their lives. Maybe Ma's anger and sadness would have faded, and they could have reconnected. But Frankie hadn't stuck around to give it a chance. She'd assumed that with Ma disowning her and with Dylan getting married, her world as she knew it was crumbling. It hadn't even occurred to her to try to make it work.

She had been in pain, and she didn't want to feel that pain anymore. So she left.

And now she was doing the same thing. She'd left town and she'd turned her phone off so she wouldn't be tempted to call Dylan. Sure, she hadn't fled as far this time, but she was still running.

On the second part of the loop back toward Wing Keung's house, she sped up. When she got there, Shirley was in the kitchen, making tea.

"Would you like some?" Shirley offered.

Her first thought was to say no, but she had so many thoughts racing through her head that slowing down for a moment would be nice. "Yes, please."

Shirley poured her a cup and the two of them moved to the living room to sit on the couch.

As she watched the steam curling away from the tea, Frankie said, "Shirley, can I ask you something?"

"Of course." Shirley looked at her expectantly.

"How did you know you loved my brother? How did you know you wanted to spend your life with him?"

Shirley put her mug on the table and clasped her hands as she leaned back and smiled. "It was simple, really. I couldn't imagine myself with anyone else. And I didn't want to."

Frankie frowned. "What about when he does or says something you don't agree with? Something that hurts you?"

Shirley pursed her lips in thought. "That's part of relationships, I think," she said after a moment. "Even when we love someone so deeply, we have disagreements, or we say things that hurt each other. But sometimes those arguments can push you to be a better person."

Frankie nodded slowly, a plan forming in her mind. "So the arguments are worth it?"

Shirley laughed. "Of course they are. If you don't accept the ugly pieces of something, you miss all the beautiful pieces as well." Everything Shirley said confirmed what Frankie had thought about on her walk. She was reminded of what Margie had said about fighting for Dylan.

"Do you mind if I borrow your car?" she asked Shirley. "There's something I need to do."

"I don't mind. The keys are on the side table."

As Frankie left the room, Shirley called, "What about your tea?"

"I'll microwave it when I get back," Frankie said over her shoulder. Although if her plan worked, she might not be coming back right away. "Thank you!"

Before Frankie grabbed the keys, she went upstairs to the guest room and pulled out the worn copy of *Pride and Prejudice* from her suitcase. She flipped the cover open, sliding out the fortune.

Love is the only true adventure.

Frankie was starting to think the fortune was right. She'd been on many adventures in her life, but none of them felt anything like loving Dylan. None of them were as exciting, as thrilling, or as fulfilling.

It was time to go after the adventure she'd been afraid of.

She didn't want to run anymore.

CHAPTER THIRTY-SIX

DYLAN

As soon as Samaira left, Dylan called Evvie to tell her the news. "Are you serious?" Evvie practically screamed through the phone. Once she had calmed down, she said, "I have news too."

"You do?" Dylan bounced in place.

"Mm-hmm. I quit."

She stopped bouncing. "What?"

"I gave my notice at the clinic. I'm retiring."

"What the fuck, Evvie? Congrats!" Then they were laughing like they'd just heard the funniest joke in the world.

After Dylan hung up, she ran up and down Main Street to share the news with her friends. She couldn't contain her excitement, her whole body vibrating.

They closed the library at five o'clock and convened in the diner to celebrate. Jamie ran to the Juniper Foods liquor store for bottles of champagne, and Aaliyah brought over a cake for everyone to share from the bakery. Dylan, Evvie, Minnie, and Eleanor sat at a table together, laughing and drinking their champagne. Warmth bubbled up in Dylan's chest, and she was pretty sure it wasn't from the alcohol.

The only thing missing was Frankie. The cake Aaliyah had

brought over was chocolate, and Dylan hadn't been able to take a bite yet because it reminded her of Frankie's absence.

Her phone vibrated in her pocket, and she ignored it. It was probably a scam call anyway. All her friends were here, including Hugo and Gwen. Hugo sat at the other end of the diner, cozying up to a girl Dylan hadn't seen before. He looked happy, his cheeks flushed and his head thrown back in laughter. Gwen was sitting with her kids, trying to keep them from getting chocolate all over themselves.

Her phone vibrated again, and she sighed, pulling it out of her pocket. The name on the screen just about stopped her heart. It was Frankie.

"Evvie, move," she said, shoving at her friend so she could get out of the booth.

"Whoa, okay, what is happening?" Evvie got up and Dylan flew past her and out the front door to get away from the noise of the party.

She answered the call, hoping she hadn't let it ring for too long. "Hello?" she said breathlessly.

"Hi."

Dylan heard the word through her phone but also as if Frankie was standing right in front of her. Frowning, she looked around to see Frankie standing on the sidewalk to the left of the diner, out of view of the front windows.

"Frankie." Her name left Dylan's mouth like a prayer, and if Dylan was going to worship anyone or anything, it would be Frankie.

"That's my name," Frankie said, stealing Dylan's line. "Can we talk?"

Dylan nodded. "Yes, please."

"Can we go somewhere more private?"

The first place that came to Dylan's mind was right across the street. "Does the library work? I've got the keys."

Frankie followed Dylan over, and Dylan's hands shook as she unlocked the front door. What was Frankie doing back?

Dylan flicked on the lights and stood awkwardly by the wall, not sure what to do. Finally, Frankie went over to one of the comfy chairs and sat down, so Dylan did the same, sitting across from her.

"What are you doing here?" Dylan asked. "I thought you'd be in India."

Frankie shrugged one shoulder. "Let's talk about that after. I have something else to say first."

"Okay." Dylan swallowed, hard. "Shoot."

"I was upset, on Saturday. I know you were too, and that we both said things we probably shouldn't have said. But you were right. I ran because I was upset. I was actually planning to stay, I just hadn't officially decided yet, and I think I was scared of that and scared of messing up our relationship. So, at the first sign of trouble, I ran. I took it as a sign that we weren't meant to be."

She had been planning to stay? Dylan bit her lip, feeling worse now about their fight. "But . . . ?"

"But I'm not going to make the same mistake I made fifty years ago. I had a great career and a fantastic life, but I missed you. Every single day. I always wondered what you were doing and what it would be like if we reunited. I was so scared of being rejected again that I didn't even give us a chance." She laughed sheepishly and pulled a book out of her satchel, holding it out to Dylan. "I carried this with me everywhere."

Dylan reached out to take the book. "*Pride and Prejudice*?" Her cheeks heated.

"Yes. It reminded me of you. Like I was carrying you with me. I know, it sounds ridiculous."

Dylan laughed. "It doesn't." She shrugged off one jacket sleeve and pulled down her T-shirt to reveal the crane tattoo on her shoulder. "I carried you with me too."

Frankie's jaw dropped. "You have a crane tattoo?" She stood, coming over to Dylan and lightly tracing the ink on Dylan's skin, making her shiver.

"It's your favorite bird, right?"

Frankie dropped her hand. "Yes."

Standing, Dylan pulled Frankie into her arms. "You were right too. About me being single-minded. I want you to stay, and I should have told you. I shouldn't have let work override my feelings for you when *you* are what I truly want."

Frankie pulled back slightly, and Dylan linked her arms around Frankie's waist to keep her close. "You want me to stay? You want me here?"

"I do. Let me be even clearer." She looked Frankie in the eyes. "Frankie Chan, will you stay in Juniper Creek with me?"

A grin grew across Frankie's face, and she laughed. "Yes, Dylan Lavoie, I will stay in Juniper Creek with you."

Dylan pressed her mouth against Frankie's until they were both breathless. "Good," she said. She touched the tip of her nose against Frankie's and pulled her even closer for a moment, reveling in the fact that Frankie was back with her.

Frankie reached up and smoothed Dylan's hair back, and Dylan grinned at her. Then she realized where they were standing and what Frankie had missed. "Also, I have news."

"Oh?"

"Yeah." A thrill shot up from her toes. "Someone donated a fuck-ton of money to the library board, and it's more than enough to keep all five libraries open."

Frankie didn't react for a second, then she smiled again. "That's fantastic! Congrats!" Her voice sounded overly cheery. Fake cheery.

Dylan raised an eyebrow. "You've never been good at acting. You knew, didn't you?"

Frankie pulled out of Dylan's arms more, still connected but slightly farther away. "That's the other thing we need to talk about."

"What do you mean?"

"Well, you asked what I'm doing here."

"Yeah," Dylan said, drawing out the word. "I thought maybe it was because you wanted to be. You wanted to come back."

Frankie tucked a strand of hair behind her ear. "Yes, that's part of it. But also . . . even if I went back to France, I wouldn't have a place to go back to."

Frowning, Dylan asked, "What about your cottage?"

Frankie licked her lips. "I sold it."

"You what? You sold it . . ." Dylan examined Frankie's expression, her dilated pupils, how she avoided Dylan's eyes, how her brows were drawn together slightly. Why would she be nervous to tell Dylan she sold her cottage? And how was it tied to Frankie knowing about the library staying open? Unless . . .

"You saved the library, didn't you?" Dylan asked in awe. "The money came from you. From selling your cottage." She felt like she could fly, like she could hold Frankie's hand and the two of them could soar up over the town, looking at everything down below them.

Frankie stepped back even farther so Dylan wasn't touching her anymore, her arms hanging limp at her sides. "Is that alright?" Frankie asked, strangling her satchel strap yet again.

Dylan gently grabbed Frankie's hands to still them. "Why wouldn't it be?"

"I don't want you to feel like you owe me."

Dylan laughed so hard that she had tears in her eyes. At Frankie's bewildered expression, she took a moment to breathe and collect herself. "I don't." She smoothed her thumbs over the backs of Frankie's hands. "You're my Mr. Darcy, saving me from ruin."

That brought a smile to Frankie's face, and Dylan stepped closer to her, pleased when Frankie didn't step back. "I am, aren't I?" Frankie said, smirking.

Dylan wanted to kiss that smirk right off her face. "So," she said instead, "are we doing this? You and me, together for sure this time?"

"Yes." Frankie leaned in and kissed Dylan slowly, deeply.

Dylan never wanted to let her go again.

CHAPTER THIRTY-SEVEN

FRANKIE

When Frankie rolled over in bed and blinked her eyes open to see Dylan lying beside her, it took a moment to realize she wasn't dreaming. She leaned over and kissed Dylan's flannel-covered shoulder, working her way toward Dylan's neck until she stirred and mumbled something.

"Good morning, my love," Frankie said softly. "It's time to get up for work."

Dylan rolled over and flung an arm over Frankie. The weight of it was soothing and secure. "What if I want to stay in bed with you?" she said sleepily.

"I suppose you could do that," Frankie said, smiling. "But what would Hugo say?"

"He'd be proud of me." Dylan yawned, not bothering to cover her mouth. "Gwen's in this morning anyway. I can be an hour or two late."

Frankie raised her eyebrows. "Wow, alright."

Darcy lifted her head from the bottom of the bed and wagged her tail, and Bingley came around to Dylan's side of the bed, putting her face on the comforter. Dylan laughed. "I can be late, but I guess I can't stay in bed. The girls would like to go for a walk."

Frankie laughed. "Let's go then."

Ten minutes later, they headed out the front door, Dylan with Bingley's leash and Frankie with Darcy's. They walked around the pond, hand in hand, then back at home Frankie showered while Dylan made them both coffee and fed the dogs.

"Ready," Frankie said, coming down the stairs with her hair damp and tousled.

"Let's have a quiet morning, and then I'll go in." Dylan called Gwen to let her know she'd be late, then she and Frankie parked themselves on the couch, each with a coffee and a book. This was the peace Frankie had longed for, and she couldn't imagine sharing it with anyone else.

At ten o'clock, Frankie walked with Dylan to work.

Dylan kissed her at the door. "You sure you want to come in to work with me today? Evvie's going to be there again. She says she has nothing to do now that she's retired, and I wouldn't be surprised if she makes you *another* scarf."

Frankie laughed. "I don't mind. I like her. And I like being around you."

Dylan kissed her again and said against her lips, "Then let's go shelve books." Who knew that such a mundane sentence could have so much subtext?

Evvie was in the library already, talking to Gwen at the front desk. "Good morning," she sang as they walked in. "Please tell me you need another scarf or a hat or a sweater or *something*. I'm running out of knitting ideas."

"Can't you just relax, Ev?" Dylan said as she dropped her bag in her office and took Frankie's as well, putting it on the desk chair.

"What if you pretend you're on vacation?" Frankie added.

Evvie sighed. "I don't want to be on vacation all the time. Do you have something that needs doing around here? I'll even vacuum if you want."

Dylan shrugged. "No point in vacuuming when the carpet will be replaced next week. Want to shelve books?"

"If it's useful, then yes."

"You and Frankie can do that then, and I'll answer emails." She grabbed a full book cart and pushed it over to Frankie.

Frankie and Evvie moved to the nonfiction section and slid books onto shelves, and after a couple of minutes, Frankie heard the distinct *click* of a shutter release.

She turned around to see Dylan holding her camera, looking through the viewfinder at them.

Frankie suppressed a grin. "What are you doing?"

Dylan didn't suppress her grin at all. "Taking a photo of my favorite people."

"I need to pose then, clearly," Evvie said, turning around and raising a hand to gesture at the books as if she was in an infomercial. "You too, Frankie. This is your opportunity to shine on the other side of the camera."

Frankie laughed as Dylan continued to snap photos of them. Warmth filled her from her toes right to the top of her head.

They were on their next true adventure.

Dear Library Board,

Once upon a time, I met my best friend at the library. I fell in love with her, but I didn't know it back then. Circumstances were determined to keep us apart.

Of all the things to bring us back together, it was the death of a parent and a threat to the library. We thought we'd only have a few weeks together and our focus was on what needed to be done rather than on each other, but we cherished the time that we had.

In the end, the library was what made my love stay. It was the library that kept us together and showed us that we had always been right for each other even though we didn't know it.

The library gave me my life and my love, and I will forever be grateful for that.

It gave me my happily ever after.

— Dylan Lavoie

WANT MORE JUNIPER CREEK?

Sign up for Brenna Bailey's newsletter so you'll never miss a new release! You'll also get a free, exclusive short story about how Gem and Margie met with your newsletter subscription.

Sign up now!
www.brennabailey.com/newsletter

AUTHOR'S NOTE

Thank you for joining me for another adventure in Juniper Creek! I hope you enjoyed Dylan and Frankie's story. This book is my love letter to libraries. There was a library not far from my house when I was growing up, and I visited it frequently to explore the stacks. I fell in love with so many stories there, and although my home library has changed, I wouldn't be the reader I am now without libraries!

Unlike in this novel, libraries in the Fraser Valley are flourishing as of this writing. That doesn't mean they don't need your support, though. Libraries are centers of learning, growth, and empowerment, and I encourage you to visit and support your local library whenever you can!

No matter what you thought of *Of Love and Libraries*, please help your fellow readers by leaving a review on social media and your favorite reading platforms and stores. Reviews are hugely important for getting books in the hands of the right readers. Cheers!

ACKNOWLEDGMENTS

As a settler on Turtle Island, I want to acknowledge and respect the land on which I live, work, and play. For me, that land is Moh'kinsstis in the Treaty 7 region of Southern Alberta, the traditional territory of the Blackfoot Confederacy, the Tsuut'ina, and the Stoney Nakoda Nations. This region is also home to the Métis Nation of Region 3. I have benefited greatly from living here, and I strive for partnership and reconciliation with the Indigenous Peoples who have lived on these lands for millennia. I've tried my best to bring this through in my writing.

This novel exists only due to the support of many people! If I forget to mention you here, please contact me and I'll make you a batch of apology cookies.

Thank you to Grandma Linda and Grandma Jan for engaging with a stranger on the internet to help her with her book; your experiences inspired this story. Thank you also to Nicole Glentworth and Blair McFarlane, two fabulous librarians who taught me all about how libraries work.

Stephenie Mitchell and Phoebe Kwan, your feedback made this book a thousand times better. Phoebe, thank you especially for helping me develop Frankie's character and history, and for ensuring that I portrayed her authentically.

To my beta readers—Jacquelynn Lyon, Molly Rookwood, Simone D. Sallé, and Todd Aasen—thank you once again for taking the time and energy to read this book and help me improve it.

Speaking of improvements, I worked with an amazing book

coach and two hugely talented editors who I am eternally grateful for. Trisha Loehr, your evaluation helped me see what this story was missing, and now it is whole. Abby Kendall and Alicia Chantal, you helped me polish this story and make it shine.

A huge thank you to Lucy from Cover Ever After as well. Working with you is a breeze; you to bring my characters to life and create a swoon-worthy cover every time!

Finally, I want to thank all the cheerleaders and supporters who keep me sane and pick me up when I'm down. Orin, you are the love of my life. Thank you for keeping me on track and indulging in my business ideas. Mom and Dad, thank you for letting me rant, and thank you for our weekly family nights, which help me relax. Jessica Renwick, Talena Winters, and Jennifer Lindsay, thank you for bringing me into the author fold and encouraging me every step of the way.

And thank you to my readers for picking up this book!

ALSO BY BRENNA BAILEY

Juniper Creek Golden Years Series

"I Want to Hold Your Hand" (short story)

A Tale of Two Florists

Wishing on Winter

ABOUT THE AUTHOR

Image Description: Photo of Brenna smiling at the camera. She is a White woman with curly blond hair and glasses, and she's wearing a blue shirt. End of description.

Brenna Bailey writes queer contemporary romance. When she's not writing, she runs an editing business called Bookmarten Editorial. If her nose isn't buried in a book, you can probably find her out in the woods somewhere admiring plants or attempting to identify birds. She is a starry-eyed traveler and a home baker, and she lives in Calgary, Alberta, with her game-loving spouse and their cuddly fur-baby.

twitter.com/editorbrenna

instagram.com/brennabaileybooks

Printed in the USA
CPSIA information can be obtained
at www.ICGtesting.com
LVHW020024260823
756279LV00002B/43